BAKED &
BREWED

Anne Willoughby

Contents

Thank you to my husband, who has supported me through all my writing dreams.
To my mom, for all her encouragement and support over the years.
And to The Writers Sanctuary and The Red Herrings Society – thank you, thank you, thank you, because I wouldn't be doing this without you.

Chapter 1

Willow

Deadlines suck. Twenty days until my final manuscript is due. Who chooses a deadline that lines up with midterms? My flipping editor, that's who. I yell at my students for procrastinating and here I am in my office at 2 am, trying to figure out these blasted recipes.

"This may have been one of my more idiotic ideas." I grumbled as I shifted through the papers. The last two recipes were proving difficult to read, and it was going to make or break this textbook.

I heard a tinkling laugh as Tess flitted by my head and landed on my desk. She only stood about 6 inches tall, but every centimeter of her mocked me.

"So help me, I'll paper cut you if you keep it up. I haven't had near enough caffeine to put up with you. Or to keep me up until 2 am."

"We could go home and start afresh tomorrow. New coffee, new morning." Tess flicked her dark purple wings closed behind her and leaned against a book on my desk.

The words were starting to look like gibberish on the copies in front of me. My eyes felt pressure building behind them. I'd never make it to the witching hour, and I still had to teach tomorrow. Today. Crap. With a sigh, feeling every aching moment I'd sat in my desk chair, I got up and grabbed my jacket.

"Come on, let's go home. The research can wait a little longer."

I slung my backpack on my shoulder as Tess flew past me and locked the door behind me, not bothering to take anything else home. Time would fly all too quickly, and I'd be back at work anyways.

The hallways were bustling with those who were more nocturnal, and I waved at a few students heading to the computer lab or night classes. The college taught classes around the clock to accommodate students and professors from all walks of life. I mostly taught witches and humans, which meant day time classes. My office hours varied, and I had a history of staying too late which is why I recognized many of the students roaming the halls; the buildings never closed because there was everyone from vampires to humans taking classes here.

The trek out of the building and down the hill wasn't too bad, but it was chilly in the late night air, and I wished I'd brought a better jacket.

"You okay? Not too cold?"

Tess' wings flickered close by, and I could see her shake her head. "Heading that way, though. Soon I'll be cooped up again."

It was nearly October, and fall was arriving with full force. I hoped I'd actually get fall weather instead of going straight into winter. Pixies didn't do well in the cold. Historically, they hibernated. Now, they didn't always have to.

I passed my old dorm then and thought about how much fun I had had then. Parties when Piper could drag me to them, staying up late and watching movies or cramming for a test or writing a paper. Endless procrastination, and determination to do well. There were bad memories buried deep too. Memories of a certain guy who broke my heart. And then the girl who ripped the remains to shreds.

"Why did I walk to campus today?"

"Because you walk every day?" Tess said near my ear.

I swatted at her, knowing she'd dodge it. Just because it was true didn't mean I couldn't grumble. I only lived about a ten minute walk to campus, and parking was crazy expensive. If the weather was bad enough, I usually managed to find a ride in. I regretted every minute of that decision at two in the morning. But the walk was beautiful, even more so at 2 am with fairy lights strewn around the buildings.

Turning onto my street, I heard Tess shout, "Willow" as I started to cross the road. Before I had any time to react a car flew around the corner, nearly taking me out.

I slammed against something solid and warm as my body was jerked back and I fell.

"Bloody hell, what was that maniac thinking?"

"I could say the same for you. Have you heard of looking both ways?" came from beneath me, and I realized the warm and solid thing was a man.

"Oh my gosh, I'm so sorry. I didn't mean to. I did look. I just didn't–I mean," I scrambled as I tried to get to my feet.

All I managed to do was elbow him in the gut.

"Oomph." His face contorted. The light was low, but I could make out just enough to see he had a nice jawline. He sat up, shaking his head, laughing.

"I think I would have been better off in the path of the car."

Realizing I was still lying on the ground, I pushed myself up. My bag was still intact, and I was extra glad I'd left the heavy laptop and my work backpack at the college. Then I realized what he said.

"Oh, well, that's lovely. Sorry, but thanks again for saving my life." I grumbled, as I turned back to the road. Tess flitted up to my shoulder, chewing me out under her breath. Neither of us were at our best this late in the night. Though thinking about it, it was really early in the morning at this point, which was worse. I turned and looked at him again, holding my hand out to help.

He looked up at me, and took it. When our hands touched, the heat seemed to envelope me. I nearly gasped at the contact. Our eyes locked, and his eyes flashed amber. A witch.

"Not exactly safe to walk around at 2 am for anyone, you know. Only one of you can fly away." He noted, and smiled at Tess on my shoulder.

"I mean, I have my defenses. Stayed late at work, but I do it often enough." I cocked my head, looking over his dark clothes. My nerve endings were on fire, though I wasn't sure why they were reacting so strongly to a man I barely touched. I could always blame the adrenaline. "Thanks, really. I'm tired, need coffee, and really just wanted to be home asleep. I probably didn't look as closely as I should have."

"No worries. I was heading home myself. Okay from here?"

"Yep. Just across the street."

And why did I just give him a clue to where I lived? Idiot.

He nodded then dramatically looked both ways. "Wanna cross now?"

I silently cursed myself for feeling *any* attraction to a man so incredibly handsome and rugged...getting off topic, I made a point to look both ways before hurtling across the street, Tess in tow. When I turned back around, he was already gone.

"Well, that was odd."

"Being rescued, insulted, or turned on?" Tess asked me.

"Oh, why do I keep you around?"

"You like me fine when you've had coffee," she replied.

I'd already started walking up to my home, thankful to have no more paths to cross. My cottage vaguely resembled a mushroom. The roof was yellow, the house itself a gray color, with wooden shutters and stained glass windows. It was small with just two bedrooms and one bath (with one lovely clawfoot tub). But it was home, lit up with fairy lights and glowing mushrooms in the garden. I sighed, opened the gate, and went to collapse into bed.

A very annoying noise kept repeating in my ears. I flailed, trying to get it to shut up, and accidentally hit my phone onto the floor.

"That's your alarm, you know." Tess giggled on my nightstand. "Probably reminding you that you have somewhere to be."

"I realize that." I sat up and rubbed my groggy eyes. I got out of bed, found my phone, and turned off my alarm. 9 am. Suddenly it was way too early. At least I still had a few hours before I had to teach. A hot shower, all except for the excruciatingly cold water to wash my hair, and I felt like a person again. These were the mornings I regretted having my hair dyed funky colors - but then again that cold water always woke me right up.

"Coffee. I need coffee." I walked out of my bedroom and into the kitchen, staring around blankly. Maybe I should keep iced coffee in my fridge? Then I'd have to remember to buy it.

"You always need coffee. You should just make your own." Tess was wearing a black tutu skirt, holey leggings, and a black sweater. It made her look like a tiny goth witch. I loved her style.

"It's better at the café. They have a way with it."

"They use magic." She landed on my shoulder. That had taken getting used to, and I had to learn to ignore the fluttering of her wings when she sat there.

"Yes, making it extra magical to me." I loved magic. I always had. I'd dreamed of being able to do it, but sadly I was born normal. Magic was all around us – witches used it in potions and spells, but in the recent century had started using it for mundane things that they could share with the world. Coffee, baked goods, bath products. It was wonderful.

Tess rolled her eyes again. How a creature so small could do that so effectively, I wasn't sure. I grabbed my bag, and we headed outside into the still chilly morning air. The leaves were beginning to turn colors as fall took over. It was not too far into the semester, and midterms were coming up soon. I was barely ahead of grading, and ready to fall under a mountain of it again. And I had to finish my blasted research *and* the writing in... 19 days.

Coffee. Java. Wonderful Caffeine. Peppermint Mocha with an extra shot of espresso and a boost from the magic. That was what I needed. Then I'd figure it out.

I'd first discovered this magical café called "The Witches' Brew" when in college. It looked like a perfect witches' hangout, two stories of all stone and a thatched roof. A sign shaped like a cauldron hung outside, and there were tiny gnome statues in the garden that actual gnomes had gifted them. There was even a tiny sitting area for pixies, which Tess always loved.

The bell overhead rang out as I walked in, and I heard Charlotte sing-song good morning. I shook my head at my former student and started to order.

She put a large peppermint mocha with an extra espresso on the counter in front of me, along with a thimble size of hot milk and smiled.

"Hot, and fresh. Right?"

"I come in here too often, don't I?"

Tess barked a laugh, and I considered poking her in midair, damn the consequences of if she fell or took revenge on me later.

"No clue what you mean!" Charlotte's grin said otherwise, as she gave a little wave to Tess. I decided to pretend like I believed her.

I paid and was turning to leave when he walked through the door. I froze, cup raised to my mouth, and looked at the man who saved me last night or rather, this morning, wearing an apron and bearing a tray of muffins. Tasty looking cinnamon muffins.

Charlotte beamed, "Oh! Professor Willow, Tess, meet Mr. Sullivan, our new owner."

"New owner?" I asked. No one had said anything about a new owner. I came in pretty much every single day, and knew Maggie, the *last* owner, quite well. Why hadn't she mentioned it?

"Yeah, Maggie decided to retire. She sold the place. Surprised us with the news last week, then took off on a cruise, apparently. Oh, I should have told you sooner, I just... anyways."

I heard the slightest hint of a grouch to Charlotte's voice. That was something.

Then again, Maggie was good at disappearing on vacations, as the staff were well trained

."I had been wondering where she was."

"Excuse me, Charlotte," Mr. Sullivan said, as he began loading a tray on the counter. My mouth was watering and I gave in. The cinnamon smell was calling to me.

"Are those fresh?"

"They are. And fancy running into you. Glad to see you made it home okay. How are you feeling? Bruised?"

"You two know each other?" Charlotte asked, very interested.

I shook my head, terrified of the gossip waiting to follow me on campus. Bruised indeed. "No. The new owner was just kind enough to save me from being run over last night on my way home. Didn't even exchange names. I didn't realize..."

Charlotte looked depressed at that, then perked up with interest. "You were almost run over?"

I shook my head. "Idiot driving too fast on my street." I looked back at the case, and up at him. "I'll take a muffin, too. Please."

I was sore, even from just the little fall, and I didn't want to admit it.

After paying, I grabbed my muffin and waved at them. The new owner was still standing there, empty tray in hand, as I walked outside.

"Missed opportunity that." Tess seemed mightily annoyed with me. She kept flying around my head.

"What?" I asked Tess.

"I mean, just look at him. You still didn't get his first name. What kind of person ignores fate bringing you back together again so soon?"

"A tired one, with research to do, a muffin to eat, coffee to gulp, and a class on witches' literature to teach. I don't even remember his last name. Come on."

Tess stopped in midair, and shouted, "Oh! I forgot my milk. Wait." She flew back into the café. I pondered walking off, but stayed.

I stood there, breathing in the fresh air to wake up and waited. When I took a bite of the muffin, I was transported briefly to heaven. The muffin was glorious, hot, and crumbly, and everything I'd ever dreamed a muffin could be. A vast improvement over the previous items served. They'd always had great coffee–the bakery items, not so much. Perhaps I didn't mind Maggie selling so much. And then I wondered if he had been personally responsible for baking these. That'd be more important than his looks.

Tess appeared beside me, milk in hand, and smiled. "His first name is Winston. Mr. Winston Sullivan."

I quirked an eyebrow at her. "Did you ask?"

"I had a short conversation, is all."

I eyed her, but shrugged, and continued eating the muffin. It was turning out to be an okay morning after all.

"I'm an idiot. Have I mentioned that?" I said, growling over my second cup of coffee. Thank Goddess I had a pot in my office. Piper, to her credit, just laughed. I could hear papers rustling in the background, and knew that Piper was also at work.

"What did you do now?" Her voice tinged with amusement, and the knowledge she had from decades of friendships.

"I was almost run over last night, got rescued by the new owner of the Witches' Brew, ate a muffin, and thought today was going well. But I still can't make heads or tails of these last witches' recipes, I'm never going to finish this book, and I want to crawl under my desk and nap but can't because I have class in thirty minutes."

"I'm sorry, you were almost run over? And what guy rescued you?" Piper's voice notably pitched higher as she said 'run over' and I realized perhaps I wasn't giving that enough importance.

"Ah, the new owner I mentioned. Winston Sullivan, apparently."

"Is he hot?"

"Piper!" I rolled my eyes, not at all surprised that she focused on the guy first.

"I mean, what other concern could I possibly have here?"

I dropped my head onto my desk. "I was almost run over?"

"Well. Almost. And you are currently at work, and on the phone with me, so clearly all is well there. What I can't figure out is whether or not he was hot."

"Maybe."

"Hmmm. Sounds like we need to have a girl's night. I'll bring wine. And you can tell me exactly how cute he might be."

"I need to work on my book. These last two spells are giving me trouble, and I may not be able to decipher them. I don't have time to describe him to you, and debating whether or not he was hot. Just go to the café."

"While that will certainly *also* happen, I need these details from you. We have drastically different taste in men, if you haven't noticed. Take the spells home. I can try to help."

Piper was a witch so she might be able to help me decipher the spells. Time to swallow my pride, and spill the beans about whether or not he was hot.

"It was after 2 in the morning, I was so tired, and there was barely any light."

"You saw him again at the café right? Was it dark then? I can take back my offer."

"Okay. Okay. That'd be perfect. Thank you. Six?"

"Six. Give me every single detail you got – start memorizing them now."

I hung up, and gathered the stuff up for my class, not picturing a hot man wearing an apron, with a tray of heaven muffins a single time.

Chapter 2

Winston

"Shit!" I dropped the cookie sheet, and all the cookies I had just baked for the café.

I sighed in exasperation as Charlotte poked her head back into the kitchen.

"Boss?"

"Any customers hear that?"

"Nope, but I doubt they'd care. I mean, we mostly get the college scene anyways."

"Right, right." I glanced at my hand, looking at the burn which was already turning a blistering red. Turning to the sink, I grabbed the ointment Maggie had always kept near it. Good idea, that. Then I noticed Charlotte still staring at me.

"I'm fine. Just a burn. I'll heal it up quickly."

"Okay!" She popped back into the store front. She was so chipper. My aunt had not been kidding when she warned me of that.

A few minutes later, and burn free, I used a pot holder to grab the cookie sheet from the oven. The smell was heavenly, and they were ready right in time for the afternoon rush. At least according to my aunt. I was thankful she had given me so many pointers on the café before I bumbled myself into listening to her and buying it. That said, she'd also left quite a lot out.

Like a certain regular, and friend, named Willow.

The café was still empty as I filled the case up with the chocolate raspberry cookies. I left the back glass open a crack so the smell could fill up the front even more than it already had. Not everything was magic, just simple logic.

Charlotte was watching me when I turned around. Her keen eyes seemed to see every part of me. She was also a witch, and helped in making the coffee. We infused it with wake up spells, or focus spells, all depending on what the customer wants. It was noted on a sign on the counter, so no one could complain they'd not known.

"Can I help you?"

"Nope. Just learning what I can about my new owner. *Boss. New* boss. The *new* owner." Charlotte's voice picked up speed as she corrected herself.

If someone's head could explode hers might. I laughed, shaking my head.

"It's okay. What have you learned?"

Rubbing her hands over her bright red face, Charlotte collapsed onto the counter, not looking at me.

"Are you going to survive it?" I asked.

"What?"

"The embarrassment? It's fine, really."

She looked up at me, and straightened off the counter. "Well, you seem to have a good sense of humor. Oh, and you rescue women at 2 am to keep them from being run over, so a gentleman. And you bake really well."

I felt heat creep up at the mention of my late night encounter.

"I couldn't sleep in the new place, so I went for a walk..." I trailed off. She was smiling a little too broadly.

"What?"

"You seem distracted a bit today too. I mean, do bakers normally try to pick up cookie sheets bare handed?"

I growled. "No. And I'm not."

"Not what?"

"Distracted!" I was a bit louder than I meant to be.

"Then you might want to put the tray down and stop waving it about."

A customer walked in and Charlotte cheerily greeted them by name as I ducked into the back. They made a purchase and then I heard noises. It seemed like the afternoon student crowd was coming in to study. I was starting a new batch of croissants for some sandwiches, when Charlotte popped in.

"The cookies smell wonderful. Can I have one?"

"Sure. No cost, just like my aunt."

She beamed, then slyly said. "Her name is Professor Willow Redwine, by the way. The multi-colored haired woman you rescued and briefly met this morning? She teaches at the university - studies and teaches the history of magic."

"Magic? She's not a witch." Her eyes were the greenest green I'd ever seen.

"Nope. Her best friend is though. She talked about it in class."

I pondered that. "Why would a human teach magic, though? Wouldn't witches hold those jobs?"

"Usually. The rest of the department is. But she mostly teaches all of the rest of them who are curious. Plus, she's really good at it. Published several books too. Working on another one if I remember right. Frequent customer too..."

I realized I was asking way too many questions about a woman I just met. Even if I kept remembering the feel of her on top of me when she crushed me after saving her. And why that memory seemed so appealing, I had no idea at all.

"Thanks Charlotte. When do you get off?"

"I switch out with Lyzzie in about an hour. She'll be here the rest of the evening till we close. She's a pretty good baker too."

"Yeah, Aunt Maggie told me."

"Cool."

A ding went off, and Charlotte went back out to help the next person. The sound became a steady companion as I baked and assembled various sandwiches and foods. Two pots, one of tomato and one of chicken noodle soup simmered on the stove, and I doled out orders as they were called. When the afternoon rush died down, I told Lyzzie, who was the exact opposite of Charlotte in attitude and dress, to come get me if she needed me and headed upstairs.

It was odd to suddenly live above where I worked - and odder still to own all of it. My aunt had been more than nice to sell the place to me, claiming she'd planned for me to inherit and take over for her all along. She'd sold it at quite the bargain too, as she had a life savings already, and planned to cruise away most of it. This way, it saved me on inheritance tax, and she didn't have to keep up with it anymore. She could take the money and live happily ever after with it. It hadn't taken too much convincing on my part, since moving away seemed like the best idea at the time.

I checked my cell phone, and saw three missed calls from my mother, and one from my aunt.

Perfect. I called Aunt Maggie back first.

"Winston!" She screamed when she answered. I had to hold my phone away from my ear, and then decided to put it on speaker phone instead.

"Ouch, Maggie I can hear."

"Oh sorry, hang on!" she shouted, but at a lower volume. I heard a bunch of background noise, and then it died out as a door clicked.

"Sorry, sorry, I was on deck and there's music playing. Wild party, this cruise. How is the first day going?"

"Well. You were spot on about everything you told me. A few customers have been irate at your sudden departure though. Lyzzie and Charlotte coped just fine, and have been running it well so far as I can tell."

"Eh, I didn't want a going away party or any kind of fuss. They'll get over it, at least the ones who even notice."

"A professor named Willow noticed."

"Oh, you met Willow did you? Very nice girl. We've had many chats about magic. She's sweet and loves it all. I wish she had been a witch, really. I'll have to email her."

Imagining Aunt Maggie emailing anyone was an odd thought.

"How is the cruise?"

"Good, I'm having the time of my life. So glad I decided to do this."

A door opened somewhere, because I heard the loud music again, and then it died back down. It certainly sounded like people were having the time of their life out there.

I shook my head. Aunt Maggie had owned the café for as long as I could remember. Over the three decades I'd been alive, I'd spent summers as a kid running around the gardens and helping bake things in the kitchen. And eating way too many sweets. This place held so many fond memories for me, and I knew the layout of the kitchen like the back of my hand. But my mother hadn't been happy with the decision to leave California.

"Remember, don't let your mother bully you. It's a sound investment, and you needed the change."

"It's like you can read my mind. She's next. I've missed three calls."

"Well then, don't let me keep you from the delight. I'll call when I can!"

Click. She was probably off to drink more. She'd always been the life of the party.

Staring at my phone, I realized I hadn't updated my mother's contact photo in years. There she was smiling, her hair still brown instead of the bright silver she sported now, her amber eyes sparkling. I hit the green phone to call, and waited, each dial tone sending my heart beat racing higher.

"Winston!" The tone was miles away from the delight in my aunts.

"Mother. What did you need?"

"What did I need? Can I not just check in on you? I mean, you moved across the county at the drop of a hat! I wanted to know you made it safely, and ask how the first day was going. It's been nearly all day, and I called multiple times."

"Of course you can check in on me. I've just been busy figuring out and running the café, is all. Sorry, I didn't hear my phone. The first day is going well. The café is steadily busy."

"What have you been doing all day, since you weren't answering my calls?"

"Baking. Running a café?" *Saving a woman from almost being run over...* "I haven't had much time to do anything else."

"Pish posh. Get the employees to do that. Now, is there any chance you'd reconsider–"

"No."

"You didn't even let me finish."

"And I'm not going to. I am not reconsidering my having an arranged marriage. There shall not be one, period. We did not like each other, and I am not being saddled into some relationship to try and produce kids of all things, when neither of us wants it. Stop. Asking. Me."

I was met with silence at that. I knew this was the topic that she was really calling to talk about – not whether or not I had made it safely, or been enjoying my day.

"Now Winston..."

"No, mother. I am not marrying her. Not one single piece of me is considering it. You need to stop."

Multi-colored hair flashed into my mind then, and I shoved the image out of my mind.

I heard my mother snap at someone, then a disgruntled sigh.

"Spend a few weeks there. Think about this Winston. Please. You know that the witch line has a better chance if both parents are witches - and the power between you two would surely produce a witch child. This is an excellent move for everyone involved, and she's a lovely girl. She'd be a great wife for you. She might even move out there and join you in this.... endeavor."

"I don't want to discuss this any longer. Good night, Mother."

Hanging up, I threw the phone at the couch, and collapsed into the soft cushions. She'd never let it go. My phone buzzed, and I picked it up to see a call coming in. My brother.

"Dude, what did you do to Mom?" Brad asked. "She's biting everyone's head off. I regret coming to visit."

"Why was it me? She might be mad about any old thing."

"It's always you. And she had just answered your call."

"I just said I was staying here, and not marrying Sherry."

"She still won't let that go, huh?" I could hear the resigned sigh in his voice. We'd had this talk multiple times over the past few months.

"You could marry her, you know. I wouldn't mind." It was a joke but one I wish I could really implement.

"Hell no. You're the older brother. Also, are you forgetting the fact that I am already married?"

"You could always have more than one wife, right? Have all the witch kids. Make mom proud."

"Look, I wouldn't marry her either if I was single. I get it. I'll try to bring mom around. It's not like she's without grandchildren, and an amazing witch daughter in law."

I laughed. "Thanks, I needed that."

"How's the bakery?"

"Café. And great. I'm enjoying it." I fiddled with the side of the cushion, thinking about the things I still needed to learn.

"Any hot chicks?"

That made me pause. "Why?"

"That's not a no - so there is?"

I let out a sigh, "Brad, let it go. And why on earth is that your first question?"

"Not in a million years. Because you live near a college now. Who is it?"

"I never said there was someone."

Hearing how my voice shifted, he knew he had me. "Nope, who is it?"

"Just... I kept someone from getting hit by a car. She's pretty cute. She came in this morning, apparently she's a regular here."

"Saved her from being run over? Hero already; way to make a first impression. Nice."

I groaned.

"Witch?" he asked.

"Nope."

"Shit." I felt the emotion in that one word, he summed it up perfectly.

"Yeah. But apparently she teaches the history of witch-craft."

"Well... I'll leave you to tell mom about that one. Oh, here she comes. Later!"

And click. People sure did like to end calls suddenly.

I buried the phone into the couch this time, and ignored it as I went to shower, wash off the smell of cinnamon and dough. Baking was one of my favorite things in the world, but I didn't always enjoy smelling like the inside of a cinnamon bun.

The hot water was glorious as it steamed up the shower. I stood there for several minutes basking in it, before finally washing myself off, and getting out. Looking in the mirror, I saw a bruise on my shoulder where I'd hit the concrete. That would explain some of the soreness for the day. I was bone weary, tired though, and just wanted to sleep.

Thinking back to that moment, I wondered why she hadn't seen the car coming. Then again, it was going rather quickly down the small sideroad. I'd just been glad I'd reached her in time. Her multi-colored hair had been vi-brant against the night, and the pixie following her had glowed too.

Her body had felt quite wonderful slammed into mine, and when she looked at me the first time... she'd had beautiful green eyes. Maybe the friend Charlotte had mentioned had magicked them. It didn't matter. My reaction had been rather quick, but then she'd elbowed me in the gut trying to get off, and I'd had time to control myself. And stuff my foot in my mouth at the first opportunity.

I dressed, and did a few stretches with my arm. Giving in, I dug my phone out of the couch and turned on the screen.

One unread text, from mother.

"Think about it, please."

I sat down and dropped my head into my hands, rubbing at my eyes. I'd had a late night running out for supplies and items for the apartment. The bigger items were all to be delivered tomorrow. I needed to go back down into the café, eat something, and help close up for the night. Turn in early, and not sit here thinking about a woman I had no good sense going after.

Running from one relationship, avoiding another, and moving across the country to run a café I bought spur of the moment was probably enough to dwell on for anyone. Who needed to add in another relationship on top of that? No matter how cute she was. Instead, I should think about what I needed to do for tomorrow, and find out where the account books Aunt Maggie had promised me were in the kitchen to figure out the financials...

Willow Redwine. It was an interesting name. I wanted to know more about her... and I'd be sure to see her in the café again if my employees were right. I could only hope I'd see her tomorrow... and maybe strike up a conversation with her. Just to get to know my regular customers, after all. I could ask her if she liked the muffin. It was important to plan out a good menu...

Chapter 3
Willow

I considered going by the bakery on the way home to grab muffins. They'd be a wonderful treat for girl's night and neither Piper nor I could really bake anything to save our lives. And they were ever so delicious. Except I didn't want to run into Winston again. Also, they might not have muffins at this point, it really was more of a breakfast thing. What if he was making cupcakes? No, no, I really didn't need to see Winston yet.

I really wanted coffee though.

Then again, Piper was bringing wine. It was late and I really didn't need any more coffee. Time to call it quits for the night, not get muffins, and go home. That was the best idea all around for probably everyone involved. Besides Piper would be along soon and I needed to be home.

"All right Tess, let's go home."

She'd arrived about an hour ago from her job at the University library, cleaning the ornate ceilings. Tess flitted around my office as I threw scans and other notes into my bag with my laptop. She landed impatiently on my shoulder as I turned off the coffee pot.

"Let's go usually means we are going." The impatience in her voice was so solid it felt palpable.

"Ha, ha. We're going, we're going." I knew she was really worried about the temperature dropping tonight.

The walk home was quick, with the crisp autumn air gently blowing the smells of campus about me. A cookout, flowers, and... coffee. I breathed in deeply, and stopped to soak it all in. A college campus always called to me.

I felt a sharp jab on my ear.

"Are we stopping or what?"

"Ow!" I shouted at her, then realized I'd been standing across from the bakery. Oops. It looked adorable in this light, and as always I was drawn to it. The lights and sounds and smells were all just so homey and relaxing. The stone house was on the smaller side, even being two stories, and I always thought it would have been at home in the middle of a forest.

"No, we are not stopping. Next time just say something. You don't have to hurt me." I pretended to swat at her.

"I didn't hurt you." Indignance floated off of her.

I shook my head, and within a few minutes was at my house. I flicked on some lights, put my stuff down in the living room, and flopped onto the couch. I was worn out, stressed, and stuck on the repeat of saying "19 days" and then daydreaming about muffins.

Maybe I did drink too much coffee.

My door opened with a bang, and I heard, "The party has arrived!" shouted from my doorway. Turning my head, I saw Piper standing there with two bottles of wine, and a bag floating in front of her. Her hair was wild from the wind, and she looked a little crazy.

"Hello best friend." She said, moving into the house.

I didn't even move. "Hi, best friend."

"Really? Nothing?" Piper deflated, looking at me.

"It's been a long couple of days. Also, that's the third time you've done that. I sort of expected some crazy entrance lately."

Piper made a strangled noise, came in closing the door behind her, and then took her bag into the kitchen.

"Change it up. Noted. I'll do something crazier next time. Or not crazy at all. Whatever will you expect? You can't know..." She shouted from my kitchen.

I heard bangs—my pots being moved—and then water running. A few minutes later, Piper plopped down in front of me, handed me a wine glass nearly full to the brim, and said "Pasta in 40."

"Oh thank Goddess, I love you."

I took a sip of the wine, and another. Sweet Moscato, just like I liked it.

"Now. I want all the details on the man."

"Piper," I whined. "I need help on this spell."

"Man first. Book second."

"That is the improper order of things."

She raised an eyebrow and went to take my wine glass.

"*Fine*! Fine. Man first. And he has a name. Winston."

"Churchill?"

"No! At least, I don't think so."

I heard Tess shout from the other room where her small house was, then she came flying into the living room.

"Sullivan! Winston Sullivan, remember? I told you this morning. Even went back and extra sneakily got his whole name since you didn't bother."

She sent a death glare my way and settled onto the table next to Piper.

"Oh, well, I was eating a lovely muffin at the time." I replied, trying not to laugh at her.

"You and food." Piper said, shaking her head.

"Says the woman who is cooking for me. Okay, he owns my café. He's tall, dark brown hair, rather muscular by the feel of him, tanned, flashing amber eyes. Makes excellent muffins."

"Your café? Since when did you own it? More important, by the feel? What feel?"

"Well, I mean, I did practically crush him when I fell on top of him instead of into a car head on. It wasn't an intentional feeling... I just felt him. And by mine, I mean my favorite café, the place I always go."

"Why don't these things ever happen to me?" Piper went to the other side of my couch and flopped over, her own wine glass in hand.

"I'm sure your time will come to be almost run over by someone in the middle of the night and mysteriously saved."

"I can only dream." Piper waved her glass in the air, and tried to look mystic.

I shook my head, and took a sip of wine. Piper spoiled me in her choices. That and we had similar taste.

"Do you think we can look at the book now?"

"Oh no, that is not nearly enough context or clues. Work after gossip and food. Don't you know the proper order? Spill it. Tell me everything about him."

Tess flittered by and landed on the back of the couch. I gave in and started relaying the past day and what had happened, as Tess filled in details here and there. I rolled my eyes more times than I could count, but we made it through everything.

"So to sum it up," Piper said, "he owns a coffee shop, and is apparently hot to boot. He can bake, which honestly with the way you eat should be the only thing you care about. Date him."

"It isn't that easy. And he's a witch."

"Oooooo, the plot thickens. You love witches, shouldn't that help? If not, can I have him?"

"No."

I realized what I said, and immediately buried my head in a pillow.

"Oh! You do want him!"

"I did *not* say that."

"You might as well have."

"No, that isn't..." I sighed and gave up. "Fine, I think he's hot. And yes... I may have dreamed about it. Or day-dreamed nonstop about him in an apron with a tray of muffins."

"Was it only an apron?" Tess giggled and decided at that opportune moment to fly off out of reach. Lucky her.

"So what's holding you back? You like him."

"I literally just met him, and know almost nothing about him?"

Piper waggled her wine glass back and forth in front of my face. "And that's what you learn while dating. I need to check the food. Side note – you don't have to know anything about a person to do naughty things."

She disappeared into the kitchen, and I shook my head, taking another sip of the wine.

I hollered into the other room. "Can we get down to why I actually invited you here?"

"What, you didn't just want me to cook for you? I thought I invited myself to learn about the hot guy. You had no part in this!"

"Well, I mean, besides that, I agreed to it."

Piper laughed, and rejoined me on the couch. "Fine, fine. Spells. Let's look."

"I cannot figure out these last two recipes. I have the rest of the book ready to go, but I don't know what to do with these. And I promised a certain number to my editor, so I worry about backpedaling."

"Okay, if you won't let it go until after dinner, let's see what you're working with."

I pulled out the copied papers from my backpack, careful to set the wine far away from them. They were copies of the original grimoire pages, or so I thought. Even if it had been bound as a normal recipe book and made to look like one. Every other item in the cookbook had turned out to be an old remedy or potion for ailments and issues commonly given. These two, I couldn't make heads or tails of.

"You know, I don't like making potions. It's not one of my strong suits. Hell, I barely can put together some of the basic ones."

"But you are so good at cooking. That makes no sense at all."

"Potions take patience, on a whole other level. Practicing while making. Cooking is just food coming together to taste good. If it doesn't work, you just have a whole mess of something inedible. Mess up a spell? Boom."

I shook my head, remembering how she had nearly blown out the whole wall in their kitchen. I certainly had never forgotten it, or the look on Piper's mother's face. Piper was right in that her potions often turned wrong and her mother quit letting her practice in the house.

"Okay..." Piper studied it carefully. "I can read a few of these, but I have no idea what it means. This seems like another language."

I growled in frustration, and leaned back into the couch.

"That's my problem. Some of the ingredients match older names for things I know. I mean, I've been research- ing this stuff for years. I should know it. If you can't even figure it out? What then?"

Piper sat back and mused over the glass of her wine.

"Let's eat, and drink more, and take another stab at it after a good movie."

I shrugged, and carefully put away the pages to keep any accidents from happening. Trust Piper to think food, wine and time would lead to their own magical remedy. I decided to launch myself into girl's night in the hopes of forgetting my problems for at least a little while. It worked. Mostly.

After dinner, and dishes, we both collapsed. Piper was a bit tipsy, and Tess was snoozing on the arm of the couch. I took another sip of my wine, and laid my head back against the couch. I figured I should probably quit drinking at this point; I'd lost count at how many times Piper had filled up the glass before it was even empty.

"You aren't watching the movie!" Piper said, intent on a man dancing across the stage on my TV.

"I'm too stressed to enjoy it right now."

Piper gasped. "Too stressed to enjoy a musical?"

"I have so few days left to figure this out, and write the chapters based on them. And I'm clueless."

"Isn't the guy a witch?"

"Guy?"

"Your café guy."

"Oh. Um. Yes."

"Ask him."

"Ask him what?"

"How drunk are we?"

I shook my head. "Piper, ask him what?"

When no reply came, I opened my eyes and looked over at her. She smiled.

"Ask him to work with you on the recipes. He's a baker. *And* a witch."

I stopped mid-movement with the wine glass to my lips. Well. That did make a certain bit of logical sense. He would have a good background for it. Heck, as a witch he might specialize in potions...

"Most witches think I'm ludicrous though."

"That isn't true." Piper said, then paused. "Well, I mean. Mostly? The ones who know you like what you do."

"I'm a human, researching magic, which I can't even do. They think it'd be better for one of them to hold my position."

"The thing is, none of them want to. Who wants to study boring old texts all day when we could be doing all the fun things we do?"

I shook my head. There had been pushback on my joining the magical history programs, every single time. But, I'd always prevailed with my research and knowledge. And Piper was right, not many witches wanted to teach their history in the first place.

"I could ask him, I suppose. That means talking to him though."

"Oh, I can go with you! I'll ask him. We can go get coffee tomorrow."

"I think that's a bad idea." Scenarios of Piper meeting Winston paraded through my tipsy head and every single one of them ended in some kind of disaster, mostly for me.

I swirled the wine in my glass, feeling fuzzy as I watched it twirl. Piper hiccupped and giggled. I hadn't been this tipsy in months. The thought of unleashing Piper this early on Winston rang all the alarm bells I had left.

With a glance over, I realized it was pointless to argue. She was asleep, wine glass in hand, smiling serenely. Probably dreaming of some celebrity. I put the wine glass on the table with mine, and threw a blanket across her. Remembering that Tess was asleep on the arm of the couch where she'd been watching the movie with us, I moved her to her own house.

It was an old dollhouse, one of those big mansion ones that we had found and fixed ups. Tess had never liked the other bedroom, because it was just too big for her to feel comfortable in. So we'd cleaned out the hall closet, and taken the door off. The house sat in there perfectly, and Tess had made it her own. I gently laid her on her bed, and turned off the lights.

After making sure the door was locked, I flopped over on my bed with all the intent of changing....

And woke up to sunlight streaming through the window, and Tess flitting about my face.

"Ah, what?" My head suddenly swam, and I moaned, grabbing it. I felt my bra stab into my side when I moved, and looked down. I was in bed. Fully clothed. I saw Tess fly off, and then heard a loud expletive from my living room. Piper. Shit, we fell asleep after getting drunk, apparently. Tipsy? Drunk? Exactly how much had I had?

Thank Goddess it was Saturday morning, and I didn't have class today. I never got this drunk, what had I been thinking?

I pushed myself into sitting up and then realized that was a worse idea. I almost vomited, as my stomach proceeded to do nine flip flops and a few cartwheels. I gently laid back down and closed my eyes waiting for the world to stop spinning.

"Willow?" I heard Piper moan from the living room.

"Please, please tell me if you have some of that wonderful elixir?" I asked without moving.

"What?"

I moaned, unable to raise my voice anymore. I felt Tess fly across my face, the sound of her wings flapping nearly like thunder to my sensitive brain.

"She does. It might take a few minutes to make it in here though." I heard a giggle, and then felt air from her wings as she flew off again.

"Tess, watch it, or next time I'll get you drunk too." Realizing I was whispering, she probably didn't even hear me. Oh well.

Pixies could get drunk off nectar. It was rather funny to watch.

About five minutes later, I heard Piper swear again, but closer this time. I opened my eyes, and saw her in my doorway. She shook her head, took a swig of water, and stood up straight.

"All right. Your turn."

"Does it still taste disgusting?"

"Yes. It's the price for being stupid enough to get so drunk."

I sighed, and sat up, slowly this time. The world only spun a little. I took the offered bottle, and Piper's water. Then I took a hearty swig of both, one right after the other. It was the only way to keep from vomiting.

After a few minutes, I felt my stomach settle, and my head ached less. Piper flopped onto the bed beside me.

"Can we just go back to sleep?" she mumbled against the pillow.

"Ugh. You can, but I want to shower. Maybe. In a few minutes."

The elixir worked wonders, but it took a bit to fully help. I finally stood up and started towards the shower. I had the water running, and was naked, before I realized I hadn't grabbed clothes. Oh well, Piper had seen me in worse states. I'd just wrap the towel around me.

The shower water was hot, and did wonders on my brain. I had to drop the temp to wash my hair, which did a great job of waking me up. Not as great as coffee, but it worked. As I got out of the shower, Tess showed up, buzzing about. She had changed as well, and fixed her hair.

"Have good dreams?"

"None that I remember."

"Well you were talking quite a bit. Or should I say moaning."

"What?"

Tess laughed and then took off. Moaning? About what? Then, realization hit me about what kind of moans Tess would find funny, and my entire face went scarlet in the mirror. And I couldn't remember any of the dreams—what a waste.

I wrapped my hair up, and walked out into the room. Piper was curled up on the bed, asleep again. I shook my head, and went to my closet. I started to grab some ratty old sweats but then remembered that I was going to the café. I stared at my closet in panic. Finally, I selected some nice jeans, and a black top.

Black always worked right?

"Is that what you are wearing?" Tess flew in again. She was wearing a neon pink top, with a black tutu skirt. I envied her tiny fashion.

"What's wrong with it?"

"It's just so plain."

A pillow went flying, missing Tess, but making her fly higher.

"Hey!"

"Shush. You know how she is."

I turned to see Piper, sitting up and smiling.

"Sleeping Beauty awakes."

"Ha. I'm sure. I'm stealing the shower. And clothes. I feel horrid. Then we'll go to the café and you can introduce me."

"I don't even know if he'll be there!"

"He just bought the place and lives above it right? I'm sure he's there."

I had completely forgotten that Maggie had lived above her café. Oh, that made sense. He'd be there all the time. I felt panic.

"Maybe I should change..."

Twenty minutes later, Piper was dressed in a simple black maxi dress she had stolen from my closet, along with who knew what else, and we were on our way to the café. I had not changed, but had braided my hair up, and put on some jewelry. Tess had flown ahead, eager to not miss a minute. Or so she had loudly declared.

Friends were just wonderful, weren't they?

Chapter 4

Winston

The bell dinged overhead, and I looked up to see Willow walking through the door with the pixie, Tess, and someone else. I quickly looked down, and kept stocking the bakery case. Charlotte perked up immediately.

"Professor Willow! How nice to see you. And Piper, how are you? Tess?"

Tess flew about Charlotte's head and finally landed on her shoulder laughing.

"Oh, we are just wonderful."

That sounded slightly sarcastic, or maybe just a little too chipper. I looked over to see Willow coming up to the counter, but her friend Piper kept walking right past her, and up to ... me.

"Hello there..." she nearly purred at me. I smiled back, unsure what this was about, but determined to treat them like other customers.

She was taller than Willow, with wildly curly hair... and amber eyes. So this was the witch best friend that Charlotte had mentioned.

"Hello. Do you want a treat?"

Piper's eyes nearly glinted.

Realizing what I said, I stammered, "I mean from the bakery case?"

"Oh, I'll take a treat." The smile on her face was nearly enough to make me run back into the kitchen and hide.

"Piper!" Willow whispered it, but I could hear the violence promised in it.

"What? I just want a muffin. That's the treat I meant, right?" She paused looking at Willow, and then faced me, her eyes nearly sparking with mirth, "What do you suggest?"

I tried not to laugh at that, realizing that Piper was watching out for her friend.

I pulled a raspberry white chocolate muffin out of the shelf where I had just stocked it.

"These are fresh! Just made 'em."

"He owns a coffee shop. And bakes. And..." The look she gave me made me feel like I was on display instead of the baked goods. With the last pause, she had turned to look at Willow and I couldn't see her face anymore. I shook my head, wondering what that meant.

"Normal order, Professor?" Charlotte at least, was sticking to business. Though she sounded way too amused.

With a sigh, she responded, "Yes please. And a muffin. To stay for once. We'll have breakfast here. And milk for Tess please, with some honey?"

Tess took off from Charlotte's shoulders, flitting about Willow's head.

"Of course!"

They were rung up and paid, and went to sit at a table near the garden windows. I pulled out another muffin and asked, "What's the coffee order?"

"Oh, she likes a peppermint white chocolate, hot, large, with an extra shot of espresso."

"How much coffee does she *order* that you have it memorized?"

Charlotte raised an eyebrow. "She's a college professor. I think it's, like, mandatory that they live on the stuff. Also, I've worked here for over a year—I have a lot of orders memorized."

Shaking my head, I made the drink and took the tray from Charlotte.

"I got this." I turned, grabbing the cup, and started making Piper's order too.

She quirked an eyebrow at me, but didn't say anything as another customer came in. After getting the coffee ready, I threw some extra sprinkles on top of both. I started walking towards the two women, and saw that the table had been covered with papers once I reached it. I raised an eyebrow and stood there with the muffin and drinks for a couple of seconds before they noticed me.

"Oh, Winston. Sorry." Willow pushed some of the papers in a pile to make room. While she did she said, "Or well, Mr. Sullivan? I'm sorry, we've barely been introduced. I shouldn't assume."

Smiling, I looked down at her. "Call me Winston. Plus, I hear you come in here often."

I set the drinks down, with the muffin as well. Piper had already eaten half of hers.

Willow blushed, making me think thoughts I shouldn't, and said, "Call me Willow, then."

Piper was waving her hand at me, and towards the muffin. "That is one fantastic muffin. Do you use any magic?"

I quirked my lips, "Did you sense any?"

"No, but one witch to another, I can't believe you could bake that wonderful without it."

Laughing, I shook my head. "No magic in that. Though I am thinking about toying with a line of magical foods. Right now it's just the coffee."

Tess flittered up in front of my face, "Oh, maybe like love potion drinks? That would be fun."

"Tess!" Willow nearly shrieked, then coughed. "A drink isn't food. Also, love potions are fake, right?"

Piper and I agreed at the same time, "Yes."

Changing the topic, I asked, "I heard you're a professor of magical history?"

Willow looked past me at Charlotte. I didn't dare. I just smiled.

"I am, yes." She replied, looking unsure.

"But you're not a witch."

Piper laughed at that, and then took a sip of coffee.

"No, I'm not." I heard a thunk, and wondered if she'd kicked her friend under the table. "But I grew up around it and always loved it. I've done a lot of research, and I earned my position."

"Speaking of which..." Piper said, gesturing to the pile, "She has a question for you."

Willow had been about to drink coffee, but instead glared daggers at her friend.

"Question?" I was very curious now, and worried she thought I was offended at her teaching magic.

Looking down at the table, and then back up at me, she shifted in her seat.

"Well. How to put this..."

"Oh, come on." Piper was clearly ready to talk. "She's researching what she's proven is an old grimoire and can't make out some of the pages. She needs to finish it quickly, because her agent is expecting the book soon. We were wondering if you could help."

I looked from Piper to Willow. I raised an eyebrow in silent question.

"Yeah. That's the question." Willow finally relented.

"Why me? What do you need help with exactly?"

"It's an old recipe book. Or at least, that was what it was made to look like. It was actually a book full of spells and potions. And I mean old. Like the 1200s. I found it a long time ago, but it's taken ages to figure out enough of them to piece together and prove what I thought it was. And to get an agent to take it. There's two left that I really want to decipher, and we've had no luck. They were tucked into the back of the book, on much older paper, with far more elegant writing and designs."

I glanced at Piper again, and raised an eyebrow, "You can't help?"

Piper wiggled her fingers, "I don't like history, and potions are not my strong suit."

"Why me?" I asked again, looking back at Willow. The blush hadn't left her face, and her hair was a bit rumpled from where she must have run her hands through it.

"You bake? You seem good with ingredients. We just thought... well it was Piper's idea."

Tess was sitting on the table now, and she started to say something when Willow nearly knocked her over with a piece of paper. She let out a string of tiny words I chose not to hear too closely.

"Can I see it?"

Willow handed me a few sheets of paper. They were scans, it looked like, of a very old book based on the style. The writing was cramped, tiny, cursive. Images were drawn all around the page, beautifully illustrated, yet so faded they were hard to make out. But I recognized a few of the things listed on it, and saw the different amounts for each thing, much as you would see in a recipe or potion. It did make me curious.

"When do you have to have it by?" I tried not to sound too interested.

"Well... Um. It's due in 18 days, actually. So really as soon as possible because I also have to write a chapter on each of them. I can do that pretty quickly, really, but the sooner the better."

I looked back down over the pages. It would be fun to play around with potions again. And the thought crossed my mind that I'd also be spending more time with Willow to do this. That seemed like a nice perk.

"All right. You can come by tonight after the café closes. We can meet here to work on it."

"Really? Oh my gosh, thank you! I can put a plug for the café in my bio or the dedication!"

I shook my head. "Let's just see how it goes. A lot of this is gibberish. I'm making absolutely no promises."

Handing the paper back, our hands touched, and I felt a spark. I nearly dropped the paper, but Willow just set it back on the table. I thanked them again, avoided looking at Piper's face, and headed back into the kitchens.

What exactly had I gotten myself into?

Willow and Piper stayed in the café for most of the morning, before Piper took off, and left Willow pouring over her papers. She grabbed a sandwich at lunch, what had to be her third cup of coffee, and went back to the table. Tess got some water, and I saw Willow give her some of the sandwich. Then I saw her fly out one of the open windows.

"Maybe we should switch her to decaf." I suggested it to Charlotte.

Charlotte raised an eyebrow, "She would eat out your eyes as soon as she took a sip."

"She'd never know."

"Trust me on this one? Yes. She would. Your aunt tried multiple ways to make her cut back on her caffeine addiction. None ended nicely."

I huffed but went back to working in the kitchen. There needed to be some soups and other items ready for the dinner crowd. My aunt had never served that much in terms of real food. Sandwiches, some soups, occasionally something more like a meatloaf. But cooking had never been her real love, just coffee and the people. She had told us stories all the time growing up about her regular customers. I was surprised when she decided to up and sell it to me on the cheap to go travel.

I hoped after getting to know the customers, I'd be able to add more of a variety of items. Mostly, I knew it was college students, though several professors who lived in the area came by for a coffee. There were a few writers who often stayed for a few hours, working on things. So, cheaper, easy fare would go over the best. According to Charlotte, Willow lived close by. In that, she'd been right, as I discovered her home when I rescued her from the car.

The cooking and baking soothed me. I enjoyed the mixing of recipes, following each item as it transformed. Creating something new out of something that could go a thousand different ways. I also liked to mix the different coffees. Perhaps I'd have my hand at creating a few new ones. Who really needed Pumpkin Spice, anyway?

I went back out around 4 pm to see that Willow was still there, Tess sitting on the table in front of her, huffing. I began to think she planned to stay all day until I closed. We were only open till seven. That was still a long day of work, on a day that was supposed to be her weekend. She either really liked it, or really needed it to be finished. Maybe she was afraid I'd take off without helping her. Though she barely glanced my way.

I was filling up the case with the last of the sandwiches, when I heard Charlotte moan. Turning, I found her leaning against the wall, looking three shades paler than normal.

"Charlotte? Are you okay?"

She nodded, then made a funny noise.

"That doesn't sound okay."

"My brain..."

"Your brain?" I think my voice went up an octave. I heard a chair scrape, and then Willow was there.

"Charlotte? Are you getting a migraine?"

She nodded again, just slightly. Willow helped guide her to a chair in the corner, to sit down. The next thing I knew, she was in the kitchen, then running back out with a glass of water, and a damp paper towel. She placed it on Charlotte's neck, then urged her to drink some water.

"Sorry," Charlotte muttered. I walked closer to her.

"Migraines?" I asked, still a bit confused.

"I get them, occasionally. This one hit hard, and all of a sudden. I'm usually good about watching for the signs... but..."

"No worries. I didn't know you suffered from them."

I realized I had a potion that would help her. My mother and I had made them because she suffered from them badly before she hit menopause, and even worse during. But Charlotte couldn't watch the counter like this, and I couldn't leave the potion while brewing it...

Willow looked up at me, and I smiled, a sudden thought occurring to me.

"I can make something to help her, if you can watch the counter?"

"You'd trust me to do that?"

"Charlotte likes you. Plus you asked me for a favor, so I assume you won't screw me over."

Willow sighed deeply. "I had hoped to have escaped retail."

Charlotte mumbled under her breath, and Willow laughed a little.

"All right." Willow said, looking determined. "Charlotte, let me know if you need something. Put your head down, you are in no condition to drive or try to go anywhere. Give me your phone, and I'll text your girlfriend to come get you." Then she looked up at Tess flying above her, "Tess, you watch her." Then those eyes pierced me, "Winston, how long will this take?"

"Ten to fifteen minutes, depending." I turned back to Charlotte, "On a scale of one to five, how bad is it?"

"Ten." Charlotte answered.

I looked at Willow, worryingly, "Fifteen minutes. Know your way around?"

"Yep. Go."

I hurried back through the kitchen leaving Willow to take care of the customers, while I headed up to my apartment. I had everything there I would need. I'd rather brew it in my kitchen than chance putting something in the café while it was open. Opening my door to my living room, I hurried to the small kitchen. My aunt figured if she ever needed to bake or cook anything large, she'd just use the bigger one downstairs.

I grabbed a few vials, and a pot. Washing my hands, I thought intently on what I wanted to accomplish. Then I put the pot on the stove, and lit the fire with a wave of my hand. Slowly, I began to add the different ingredients. When the potion turned clear, I knew I had remembered it correctly. A strong scent of peppermint wafted from the bowl, and I knew my apartment would carry that scent for days.

I poured it into a small bottle, and hurried downstairs. Charlotte was still sitting there, trying to drink her tea, as I carried the bottle over.

"Do you trust me?"

"Of course." She whispered.

"This is potent stuff. One swig, and the pain will be gone, but it will leave you a bit weak."

"But the café..."

Willow approached at that moment and made a scoffing noise. "I can take care of it. We've got you a ride home."

And so Charlotte took the bottle, and on my direction, just a tiny sip. After just a mere moment, she dropped the cloth and looked up at me, wonder in her eyes.

"Why didn't I know this existed before? I'm a witch, I could brew this. I've had so many migraines, and most of the stuff I've found barely makes a dent."

"It was my grandmother's special concoction. She didn't like sharing. That should last you a while. I can make a tea for milder ones. Maybe one day I'll sell it."

She nodded, slowly. "I can see what you mean about feeling weak. I feel woozy, but all the pain is gone."

Willow and I helped her outside, where her girlfriend had arrived to pick her up. She had walked to work from campus where her car was, and she was in no state to get home.

"You sure you'll be okay?" I asked.

"Yeah, Laura's used to this by now. I'll explain to her that I took something, just not what. Thanks."

And with a smile, she slid into the seat and was gone.

Willow turned to me, but I realized no one was in the café, and hurried back inside. Now to see how good Willow really was with customer service. I could have handled it by myself... but I wasn't going to tell her that.

Chapter 5
Willow

Now I remember why retail is hell. Honestly, higher education can have the same "customer" mentality, but at least I didn't have to remember everyone's orders, or get them to the right tables on time. I wasn't made to be a cashier or a waitress. I'd already almost spilled five drinks, and it had only been 30 minutes.

I glanced back at the hours sign, even though I knew what it said. I'd had it memorized for years, after all. 7 pm. Almost 2 hours left.

Looking back into the kitchen, I saw Winston cleaning pots. "Why are you cleaning already?"

"I have everything stocked already for the night. Just cleaning up now."

"Cleaning... I'll clean! You can come do this."

He raised an eyebrow at me and cocked his head to the side. "Do you know where anything is?"

"It really can't be that difficult to figure out."

"My kitchen. My system. I'll clean. Where's Tess, by the way? The pixie that's always with you?"

"She went out with some friends. She'll come back around this evening. She lives with me and has the territory behind my home."

He looked puzzled, but still didn't offer me anything else. The bell dinged.

I huffed and went back to the counter as another customer came to order.

"Professor Willow?"

Shit. I recognized her from one of my earlier morning classes. "Grace. How are you?"

"What are you doing here? Professorship not pay enough? Or just want a discount on the coffee?"

With a sigh, I shook my head, "Helping a friend out. The café was short. Now, what would you like?"

Fifteen minutes later, I had the orders out, and another tiny moment of air. I needed to make him let me clean. Carrying another tray might be the end of his café. Popping open the door again, I leaned against the frame.

He wasn't even cleaning.

"Seriously?"

With a look at me, Winston stopped reading the book he had in his hands at the table.

"What?"

"You aren't cleaning. You aren't *doing* anything. I'm drowning out here! I was going to switch you jobs."

"I thought I said no to the cleaning?"

I gestured around me. "Are you cleaning?"

"Oh, finished that in here."

I growled out, "Then maybe I should leave."

He snapped the book closed, then stood. "Look, I'm happy for the help. If I'd had to clean up after close, it would have taken that much more time before I could look at those recipes of yours. I could look now, if you wished?"

And with a jolt, I realized I'd left everything on my table when Charlotte had almost fallen.

"Oh!"

I took off out of the room without an explanation. I heard the door open again behind me, but didn't even bother looking around. He'd figure it out, surely.

No one had sat at the table. The café had been busy, but not packed and mostly with to go orders. I grabbed my bag, made sure my iPad and cord were still there, and my phone. I had missed texts from Piper, of course. Then I started shoving everything into as neat a pile as I could manage, and got it put up.

A hand, large and callused, landed gently on my shoulder. I felt warmth zing up and down my body. I stopped, slowly looking up at the man I knew it belonged to.

"It's okay. I'll cover the counter. You don't have to pack like someone is fixing to rip it out of your hands."

I stopped and breathed. Research could be a dangerous game. I was used to guarding my notes at the university. That and I had just left out expensive tech, with all my passwords on it, for a couple of hours unguarded. I was an idiot.

Nodding, I felt the sudden absence of his hand, and that warmth. Without it, I almost felt chilled. "I'm losing it. Maybe I am having too much caffeine," I mumbled, as I continued putting up my things, slower and with more care. Now that was crazy talk, and clearly the stress was getting to me.

Winston had walked off, talking to patrons, and greeting them. He was good at this, charming his way through his customers. I didn't have that ability. Even as a professor, I connected most with my fellow odd and quirky people. I envied his easy charm.

With my bag all messily packed, I walked behind the counter and took it into the kitchen. With a plop, I sat it on the table, and breathed in deeply. The whole room smelled like heaven. Rich spices, coffee, peppermint, and the smell of freshly baked bread. I could live in this place and never be happier. Though I suppose it would come with Winston, which might make it difficult.

Though that touch...

At that thought, the door opened again. Winston looked in and noticed my apron in my hands.

"Done for the day?"

"Do you need me? I could use the time to work more on this before I get your opinion."

Shaking his head, he said, "No. It's the calm before closing. A few more trickle in, but never in a rush. They head home with to go cups. You people and your coffee."

"You own a café. What could you possibly have against coffee?"

I heard a ding, and Winston grinned, then popped back out. With a groan, I pulled some of my papers back out of my bag, and the iPad. Loading up the pages didn't take long, and I scrolled through the grimoire until I found the last two.

I'd had some difficulty even translating the beginning spells and potions originally. For these two, the text was cursive, like the rest of the book, but written in a different hand. Loops, extra curves, and the curliest of writing. It was ornate, beautiful, and difficult. I'd wondered if maybe they had done that on purpose, a way to guard against someone who found it but shouldn't read it. The pages had seemed older, as if they had been rebound into this book. With all the time I had poured into them, I still didn't even have half of it translated, and what I had made out really didn't make sense.

I looked again at the borders of the pages. Hand drawn art surrounded every page in the book, and with careful examination, I'd discovered all the drawings related to the spells, whether it be the ingredients or the different effects. There was a heart in one corner of this page, and I wondered if this wasn't some kind of poison.

My notes sat in front of me, barely touched. My mind just couldn't find the missing details on these. I had so little time to finish these two chapters. I could publish my book without them... but they knew how many pages were in the grimoire source I had shown them, and that translated to a certain number of promised chapters. Academic publishing was a pain.

I suppose if all else failed, I could write two summary chapters on the history of magic... though some of that was already in the beginning. That was something to ponder and possibly start. There wasn't anything stopping me from even writing about what I had deciphered and the issues that lay within discovering old spells. That was actually a good idea...

My head fell back on the chair, resting against the cold wood. The warmth of the ovens and the scents were making my already tired head worse. I might just nap for a minute or two. I had time before Winston came back here...

"Willow? Are you seriously going to sleep in a wooden chair? Your neck looks cracked."

I jerked up, nearly whacking my head against the wood. Tess was flying in front of me, looking highly amused.

"Tess. Seriously?"

"What?"

Waving my hands in the air, I gestured at her. "Ever thought about letting someone know you are here without scaring them half to death?"

"Where's the fun in that?"

I leaned back against the chair. "No fun at all, I suppose. Did you have fun doing whatever you were doing?"

"Aye. Caused maximum mayhem."

"I don't doubt it for a second. Don't tell me, I best stay in the dark." Pixies were rather fond of mayhem, for mayhem's sake.

She laughed and flitted about the kitchen. "Nice place, this."

"Uh, huh."

I couldn't keep watching her fly in circles, or my head would try to beat out of my skull like Charlotte's earlier. Would Winston give me some of that potion?

My watch buzzed, showing me Piper had sent me a message.

Piper: Almost time! Good luck... and call me tomorrow with all the spicy details.

I clicked the button and said, "There will be no spicy details," pressing send, as Winston finished opening the door.

"Spicy details? Food?"

I blushed, winced, and said quickly, "It's a girl thing. Almost closing?"

Tess's cackle made me want to throw a spoon at her.

"Yep. Just have to close out the drawer and get the floor mopped, and the rest of the equipment wiped down."

"I can help with that. Just give me a minute."

With a smile, he nodded and closed the door behind him. I stretched and looked at Tess, who had settled on the table.

"Any chance you're good with a mop?"

"Got any Q-Tip sized ones?"

I flicked my fingers at her, knowing it wouldn't land, and stood. My legs nearly seized up under me, but with a few quick steps, I started feeling normal again. Maybe one last cup of coffee...

"Cleaned the coffee pot yet?" I asked as I came through the door.

Winston was stuffing some cash into a bag and turned around.

"Coffee? Really? This late?"

"Look, I had a ... night, and I won't be coherent enough to help you out. I need something."

"As much caffeine as you've ingested today, you ought to be high on it for a year."

"There is nothing wrong with drinking coffee."

"There is if you overload yourself."

"What do you have against it?"

"Besides its awful taste, and mostly placebo effect? I mean, yes, witches enhance the beans, and imbue it with extra energy, but it's still just only a certain amount. And you can build up a tolerance for it."

I gasped. Loudly.

"How dare you besmirch the name of coffee." I might have to rethink this entire endeavor. He might not be fit after all.

Tess flitted in at that moment, adding, "You've done it now."

Winston flicked his gaze at her and back to me. "What's the deal?"

"Coffee is sacred. It is life. It is the beverage of gods and Goddesses. You own a café and sell it in droves, and you don't like it?"

"I just don't see the point."

I stomped off, grabbing the mop and bucket he'd just set out. "Not everyone is a witch who can magic up a potion or spell, or afford it. There is no hope for you."

Out of the corner of my eye, I saw him raise his hand, then drop it. He shook his head and turned back to the machines. I pointedly ignored him. *What good is coffee?* How could anyone that hot think coffee was disgusting? Clearly, my body was betraying me.

With a sigh, I started mopping. He had already stacked the chairs on the tables. I was halfway done when the smell of coffee became stronger, and suddenly, there was a small cup of deep, dark, beautiful brown liquid floating under my nose.

Inhaling deeply, I propped the mop against the wall and took the proffered cup. As I took a deep sip, I looked up to see Winston watching me. The look in his eyes made me choke on my coffee.

"Oh gosh, I'm sorry. Here." He ran to grab me a napkin, and I tried to recover myself. I was simply imagining things. There had not been heat in that gaze—we'd just been arguing over coffee.

Winston came back with a few napkins and handed them over.

"Was it too hot?"

"What? Oh, no. I just... breathed in funny while trying to take a sip. It happens." Yeah, that sounded so better, and didn't make me seem like an idiot.

His eyebrow raised at that, but he didn't object. I wiped the coffee on my hand, careful to hold the cup steady. I wrapped the remaining dry one around the cup and took another sip.

"This is delicious. Better than normal. Even if it is only a small cup. Thank you."

"It's from a slow roaster. I haven't added it to the menu yet."

I raised my eyebrow. "Maybe you shouldn't."

"I thought it was delicious." He growled back.

With a smile, I replied, "Yes, but I don't want to share it."

A laugh burst out of him, and he walked off, shaking his head again. "Come on. Finish mopping, and I'll clean this last machine. Then we'll look at that book of yours."

Sipping some more of the coffee, I walked towards the counter and sat down my very precious coffee, his quiet peace offering. Then I quickly finished the room, finding motivation from deep down. I had so many questions about that manuscript, and if he could even answer a couple of them, it would help.

Tess flitted about, watching me mop.

"Don't you have somewhere better to be?"

"Nah. It's fun watching you work."

I stuck my tongue out at her and finished the last line. Pulling the mop and bucket carefully behind me, I sat them by the counter. I'd let Winston take care of the dirty water and putting them up, since I wasn't sure where that was. Also, it was heavy, and I didn't want to do it. I had coffee to finish, which I promptly grabbed from the counter. Pushing the door open into the kitchen, I found Winston drying the last of the pots and pans and putting them away. Tess flew in behind me, landing on the table once again.

She flopped down, crossing her legs, and announced, "Let's get this party started!"

I shook my head at her antics, but followed her over to the table. I'd been working on my iPad, but grabbed my laptop out of my backpack instead. I punched in my password, and my screen filled with notes and pictures that I had been looking at.

There was suddenly a wall of heat behind me, and I knew Winston was standing there. It made every hair on my body stand up, and I felt an odd, hot sense of longing. Slowly, I turned around to face him, and found him very close indeed.

"Sorry." He mumbled, without moving away.

His intense amber eyes, the ones I noticed when he saved me from that car, were watching me. But not my eyes, they were focused a bit too low for that, more at my lips.

"Ahem," Tess loudly said from the table, and we both jumped. A freezing cold bath might be just the thing for her later. Or spoiled milk.

"Right, so, what exactly are you writing again?" He asked, moving away a bit.

I sat down, and he followed suit.

"It's a textbook, about old potions and spells. The first few chapters are generalized. About the kinds of magic witches possess, and the various ways we see them used in our society. About the history of witches, and how they have helped us throughout time. The rest of it is the evaluation and analysis of this specific grimoire. I found it years ago at an estate auction. I was always convinced they were potions and spells, but most thought it was just a cookbook."

Winston was studying the cover, looking at the different pages.

"Some of these I recognize."

"Some are really common. The last few in the back were not. I think it was a witch who married into a family that didn't approve and tried to hide it. That was common, for a time. For both sides."

Winston huffed and let out a little laugh. "Oh, don't let people fool you. There are still some issues there."

I wondered at that—Piper never seemed much bothered with anything that was going on—but I knew there was an issue with witches having children. I turned my mind back to this, though. I had more pressing timelines to pay attention to.

"So, do you think I am right?"

"Of course. This was very much a spell book, and this was an easy way to hide them if you needed to. No one reads recipes very often. If you figured these out, why are you having issues now?"

"They don't follow the normal guidelines for spells. They match no others, and the writing is so faint - as well as all the drawings. I wonder if she didn't add them into the book binding to hide them. Witches pass down spells, after all."

"They do, yes. Though orally is more common."

"Oh, I know."

Winston quirked an eyebrow at me.

"Sorry. I mean, I am a professor specifically on the history of magic. I know it isn't the same—but I have some knowledge. Quite a bit, actually."

"Right. Of course. It'll be a battle of wits over something else, then."

I smiled, shaking my head.

"I understand that not all witches like the fact that I teach your history. Trust me, there were many who hated me at school. Some of my students still resent it. But I proved myself time and time again. I'm an outsider looking in. I've got a unique perspective on things you wouldn't get otherwise, right?"

"Hey, I wasn't arguing about your place here. Just trying to understand my role in it and share what I know." He smiled sheepishly at me, and I felt guilty for projecting my fears onto him.

"Right, sorry. Okay. So I have great knowledge of many spells, but what is listed here—or well, what I can make it—makes no overall sense. And they are things I haven't heard of before. I cannot make heads or tails of its purpose or the drawings.."

I looked back up to see Winston smiling at me.

"And so Piper thought of you." I was still trying to decide whether I wanted to thank her for that.

"I'm honored. We hadn't even met."

"I might have shared the story of being saved, and then finding you as the new owner of the coffee shop with her yesterday."

"Glad to know I made an impression. So baking, potions, it's all the same in terms of mixing ingredients and getting something out of it. That's always been my take on it."

Smiling, I looked around. "It can be. And it seems to be in your case."

"Shares a lot of the same practices." Winston looked around. "Some spells have been banished. It's hard to imagine that my Mother let any spells slip outside her control. Or any of the former council members."

Winston peered closer at my notes. He nearly touched them with his nose. It was funny to watch him almost go cross-eyed.

"And these are going in a book?" He asked after a few minutes.

"Ah, a textbook. It may be reformatted and shared more widely, but mostly it's something you could use in a classroom setting."

"And... do they?"

"What? Oh, yes. I have another out already."

"Why?"

"Why, what?"

"Why do you write them?"

I stopped for a second and looked up from the computer. He sat with his elbows on the table, and his hand on his face. Just watching me. It brought a smile to my lips.

"Professors have to get published for most positions in order to attain tenure. I didn't know what else to write for the first time. And I enjoy the research."

"You don't seem to enjoy this one."

"Let's not talk about that. You're tired, right? I can leave you a couple of copies. I'm usually here on weekends, anyway. I'll come in and work here tomorrow instead. If you get a moment, we can talk."

"Or you can come back tomorrow evening. I'll have help, so we won't be working. Sorry, things got messed up tonight."

"You helped Charlotte. No apology needed. Then I'll leave these here and see you tomorrow evening."

At this, I heard Tess snort. We both looked at her.

"And morning. You know you'll come get coffee."

I was staring daggers at her when Winston barked a laugh again. That sound...

He helped me clean up my mess on the table, and I handed him some scans. He walked me out the door as Tess flew into my hood on my jacket.

"It's dark. Do you need a ride home? Or someone to walk with you?"

Winston was looking around carefully.

"I walk this all the time. No worries. I'll pay more attention to fast drivers too. Night."

"Good Night."

I could feel his eyes upon me as I turned the corner, and decided to put a little more emphasis in my walk. Make a good show for him.

Chapter 6

Winston

Sunday morning dawned bright and clear. I was already awake, though. I'd gone upstairs and crashed after Willow left, too tired to even try to look at all that cramped, tiny cursive handwriting. I felt bad about it, but it was the start of the new day, and I'd have plenty of time to do so before I saw her again tonight.

After getting a round of muffins out and coffee ready for the really early crowd that came at 6 am, I'd showered and changed. I started setting the café to rights, and putting chairs down, when Charlotte arrived right on time at 5:30.

"You are a miracle worker and my new favorite person."

"What?"

"I have never recovered from such a horrible migraine so quickly. Can I buy whatever that was by the gallon?"

I smiled. "It wouldn't last that long." At the disappointment on her face, I added, "But I could brew you some fresh every week if you need it."

"Oh, thank all the deities of every religion. Thank you. I might pass this science class if I can study without my brain exploding."

She started humming and working on the rest of the chairs. I laughed to myself and went back into the kitchen. There was baking to be done.

The smell of muffins permeated the air, and I was quickly switching out the batches to cool, bake, and store. It was already 8 am, and these might be the last ones I had to whip up that morning. The Sunday morning crowd was much slower than the Saturday one, but more of them lingered. Looking out the door at the case, I saw that most everything was stocked.

There was still time before I needed to start on lunch options, and luckily, Willow hadn't come in yet. She'd said the end of the day, but Tess had been sure she'd come get coffee this morning. Then again, I had no idea when she usually woke up. I let the kitchen door shut quietly behind me, and walked over to the table where the two scans were still sitting.

The handwriting was cramped. The drawings in the corners were stark against the background. Sitting down felt like it might be a bad idea, but I did anyway. My back ached from bending over the counter all morning. There was something vaguely familiar about one recipe, but I couldn't figure out what. Pulling out a notebook from a drawer to the side, I started trying to make out different words or figure out if there were standing names that witches used to use to cover what ingredients they were really using.

An hour passed with little success. I could make out one or two words, but it was slow going. No wonder Willow had wanted some help. *How many days did she have left for this?*

I got up to stretch and check the case. Opening the kitchen door, I saw Willow ordering coffee.

"Busy morning, I see," Willow said, as she waved at me and the café.

Most of the seats were full. We were doing good business, just like my aunt promised. But I really needed to go through the accounts to fully understand what the profit margin was, what sold best, and what I was even paying my employees.

"Yeah. Late morning?" I asked, looking at the clock on the wall. Almost 11 am.

"About normal." She smiled, and took a sip of her coffee.

"Busy, but I had an hour, and I started working on the scans. Wanna come back here? I can talk while I start on lunch items. You okay out here, Charlotte?"

She held up a thumbs up as another customer came in the door. Willow came around the counter and followed me back.

Willow plopped into the seat she had occupied the night before. When I'd gotten lost in her eyes, as they sparkled in joy at what she had told me. I'd missed a portion of it. Thoughts of kissing her had danced in my head. Then Tess had spoken up. Speaking of...

"Where's Tess? And your bag?"

"Oh, I just came by for coffee this morning. I wasn't going to bug you yet. Tess is out with some of her friends."

"You know it's close to lunch, right?"

The glare she shot me might have killed me, and I instantly knew my error.

"I've been staying up late working every night and then working on the book to boot. Plus, yesterday's work was a bit more physical than I'm used to, I'm sad to say. I was bone tired. I slept through all my alarms, and Tess stopped trying to wake me up too, apparently."

"Sorry, sorry. I shouldn't have said anything. I'd have slept in if I could have."

She smiled and waved a hand, taking a sip of her coffee.

Nodding, I made my way across the kitchen for the loaves of bread I had made yesterday morning. I sliced my way through them, getting some ready for toasting, and others for simple sandwich fare. A lot of patrons here were college students. They weren't looking for fancy here. Just filling and easy. And the cheaper, I noticed, the better.

"What are your plans for the day?"

"Work on the book at home. And grade. They just turned in a set of papers. I have so many papers to read."

Willow's head laid down on the table as she pretended to sob. I laughed.

"You chose this life."

She looked up and finally raised up enough to drink some coffee.

"I did. And I do love it. It's everything I wanted, even if sometimes you want to hold giant signs up to students that flash in neon and just say 'Read the directions, damn it.' and then yell 'Read them again' once they have done it."

"That... is really specific."

"You have no idea. So, what did you find?"

"Two words. Neither much help. Willow, and bark."

"Willow bark was a common ingredient."

"Still is. Though they weren't in the same line. So there's that."

"Hey, that's more than I had. No worries. Work on it when you can, if you are still game. I'll go home and drown in coffee and papers. Ooo, maybe I could just spill coffee all over them and ... oh right, it's all digital. That wouldn't get me anywhere, except ruining my laptop. I need more coffee."

Willow looked mournfully into her cup through the tiny hole.

"Didn't you just get that one?"

"Yes, but Charlotte was making me two more. All right, toodles! I'll see you this evening."

Before I could say another word, Willow was out the door.

I realized I'd wanted her to stay longer.

The rest of the morning and afternoon passed pretty quickly. I had expected more items to disappear at lunch, but we had a few study groups come in and wipe out our cheaper options, more than I prepared for. The soups were nearly gone too. So instead of getting to look over the papers at lunch, I gulped down a protein shake and went back to work.

How did my aunt manage this alone? Could I afford to hire someone? Who cooked while she was gone on vacation?

Around 2 pm, I finally sat down to take a break and eat something real. I was busy enough, I might not be able to look at the papers again until close. Sighing, I shoved a hand through my hair and pondered my options. I could just not restock everything, but then someone might get irate. And I hated to make Charlotte explain that over and over, even though she could just say that we were out of things...

At that moment, the kitchen door swung back open, and in came Tess and Willow. I suddenly felt happier.

"Willow, Tess. What are you doing back so soon?"

"She was screaming at her computer screen and I suggested a break." Tess seemed rather smug about it.

"Ah. Grading not going well?"

"I mean, they actually aren't that bad, for freshmen. Though I've had two or three who clearly didn't read but the first couple of sentences on the instructions. Having some computer issues too. How are things here?"

"Busy. I'm sorry, I haven't had a chance to look at the papers again."

"You are doing me a favor. Don't apologize. I could help with something?"

"How are you at cooking?"

Tess's cackle could probably be heard in the café. I raised an eyebrow.

"I make a mean pb&j?" Willow said with a smile.

Looking around, I considered my options.

"You can make sandwiches. Most of them are simply stacking the ingredients, keeping clean hands, and then sealing the bags. I have a lot of it made, like the chicken salad, and then the meats and cheeses you just slap on. We don't want too many at a time, because sometimes they request things off the normal way."

"Noted. Just point me in the right direction."

The tasks went by much quicker, and Willow kept up a steady string of babble about the college and some students going. I hadn't visited my aunt here in a decade, so it was nice to hear about everything going on.

After an hour, the café was fully stocked and ready to go. It was past 1 pm, and I realized that Charlotte's shift was almost over.

"I'll be right back." Leaving Willow and Tess in the kitchen, I walked out the door to find Charlotte talking to Lyzzie.

"Lyzzie, good. How are you today?"

"Fine, Mr. Sullivan. Looks busy."

"Indeed. I may have to find more servers. You done for the day, Charlotte?"

"Yes, sir. I'll see you tomorrow morning. Remember, I'm off Tuesday!"

I'd nearly forgotten. How did Aunt Maggie make it with such few staff members?

Making sure Lyzzie was good to go and had no questions for me, I went back into the kitchen. Willow had the fridge open.

"Can I help you find something?"

She jumped almost a mile in the air. "I just, um, thought there might be muffins."

"I sold out of my muffins this morning. Though I need to bake some stuff for the evening crowd. Also, eat real food. Have you had real food?"

"I would have thought muffins were real food, unless you were feeding me plastic? Have you had a break? Or eaten real food?" She asked, closing the door. She walked over closer to me, peering at my face.

I smiled and turned my head to look at the counter. "Muffins are real food. They just aren't very nutritious. No, I haven't had a break. Maybe I can do a short one for food."

"You need to eat. You look tired. And what is it going to hurt? You have time."

She bustled me over to the table and got me to sit. I protested, but she was quickly setting a plate with a sandwich and chips on it in front of me, and a glass of water.

"Eat." She stood there glaring at me.

Smelling the food made me realize just how hungry I was. Listening wouldn't hurt anything, so I began eating, watching as Willow went back to bustling around the small kitchen, getting her own food. After a moment, I asked about my aunt.

"So, how long did you know my aunt?"

"Oh, Maggie? I met her years ago here as a student. I loved this coffee shop. We hit it off and became friends.

She had great stories and helped me with research in the past. She never once doubted me in what I wanted to do and helped me in so many ways. Maggie was a staunch supporter of how I got into my master's program, too. I cannot believe she didn't warn me she was selling the shop."

"She didn't tell you she was giving up the shop?"

"Oh, she'd mentioned it before, after a vacation here and there, but nothing definite. I was a bit taken aback. Why did she decide to leave so randomly?"

"Not sure. She decided I needed a fresh start, and it was perfect timing. Next thing I knew, I'd agreed to come out here and take over the café, and she was sailing off into the sunset."

"Why did you need a fresh start?"

Willow was standing beside me, her own sandwich in her hands, eating. I looked up at her and thought about answering. But I couldn't. Not yet. I didn't want to talk about it.

"Doesn't matter nearly as much as finding out how my aunt did it all. She barely has any staff!"

"Oh, she always hires new students at the start of the term, but I don't think she ever did this go round. I know Charlotte has been picking up a lot of extra hours. I'm not sure why she hadn't really hired anyone."

I shook my head. "I don't think I can keep the place open with just the few I have. I at least need some people trained for backup."

Willow pulled out the chair next to me and plopped into it.

"Anyway, thanks for making me eat. You were right. I needed it. Now, I must get soups going, some new breads making, and dessert in the ovens. Then we can look at the recipes."

The rest of the afternoon was a blur. I had to go relieve Lyzzie a few times for her breaks, and Willow helped out once or twice during the rush. Otherwise, it was a large streak of baking and creating. I explained things to Willow, and she seemed fascinated by all the different items I could bake without looking at a recipe.

"How do you remember all of these?" She finally asked, as she measured out some chocolate chips based on my directions.

"I always loved baking. And potions. It's the mixing of it all and making something new. I just remember them when I need them."

Willow shook her head, then paused. "I guess it's a lot like remembering all the things I need to teach. When you do it by rote so often, it's just engrained. Even so, there is much that could go wrong here. So many things that go into one recipe."

"Hey, maybe then I'll create something new."

Once I was finally done loading up the case in the storefront, Willow and I sat down at the table. Willow grabbed her laptop and set it out; I looked for my notes.

"Why a grimoire when you can't do magic yourself?"

"Because sometimes those outside it are the first to see its value. I have always loved magic. I've appreciated it since I was little and I was watching Piper perform different spells. There was a time I hated her, because she had something I wanted so badly."

Willow shifted through notes on her laptop, not making eye contact. I started to reach out, but held my hand back. I didn't know her that well. Why did I constantly want to touch her?

"I hated magic when I was little. I was sure that I wanted anything but. My mother was so strict in our practice. I just wanted to play with my friends from school."

"My mom wasn't around much." Willow replied. Then she pulled up a great scan of the first spell.

"I know this still isn't the best, but I used a high res scanner. You can see here that these seem to be different leaves. They might refer to something within the pages themselves. I also think that it will help us figure out some of the more illegible words. Past that, I haven't managed to figure out a lot."

Tess chose that moment to swoop in between us as we were looking at the page. Or well, Willow was looking at the page. I was looking at her.

"Tess!"

"It's okay," I said, waving at Tess. She waved back.

"Willow," Tess said, flying in front of her, "We were supposed to check out the garden today."

Willow waved a hand. "We still have plenty of time for that. Besides, you have your house. You won't freeze this winter."

"That isn't the point, and you know it."

Willow huffed, and I turned a curious face to her.

"We need to go over the garden and grounds before winter hits. Most Pixies hibernate in some area of their own garden during the winter. Tess comes in my house though, and sleeps in what was basically a doll house I fixed up for her. She still needs to stake and reclaim her territory, though. I do it with her, since I don't usually pay them much attention."

"I'd heard that. Pixies aren't fond of most of California, so I haven't seen many. You'd like the sunshine, Tess."

"Sunshine, yes. The heat and ocean? Not so much." Tess landed on the table across from me. "So, are we going?"

Willow looked down across the scans, and then back to Tess. "Give me ten minutes. I can always come back, after all."

Wings beat, and I realized Tess was leaving the room again. I had been going over the items in the recipe, trying to determine if there was much hope in reading them.

"What do you do with the recipes once you have them? Since you can't perform the magic?"

"Well, Piper or one of the other witches have helped me before if I needed it made. Usually there's a description of what it's for in a roundabout way, or I've pieced it together by what the ingredients do. I have many botanist books."

"No luck this time?"

"Not yet. Being able to read the recipe first would be helpful. I thought about asking some of the other witches in the department, but didn't. I mean, they are nice to me, don't get me wrong. But academics can have a dark side, and I didn't want to give anyone leverage. Or have them demand credit."

I nodded, pretending to know what she was talking about.

"So, what credit do I get?"

She shook her head, pensively chewing on the pen she had in her hand. "Your name could go on the acknowledgements? You aren't really going to be writing anything. Or I could put a thank you note in the front?"

"Willow?" I said, a smile on my face, "I don't care. I don't need my name in the book."

She looked up at that, shock apparent on her face. "I'm sure it could benefit the café somehow..."

"Then thank the café for the writing space. Now, come on. We've barely touched this in two days, and I offered to help. Let's use the little time we have now."

Her face paled, and she looked back down at her notes. After a few scrolls on her computer, she handed it over to me.

"Is it this hard to read on the original? I wondered after looking at the scans you gave me last night."

"Worse. I've raised the contrast here. It's so aged. The pages themselves are brittle, and I worry when I handle them. I may have missed something in the scan, so it's worth looking again, but I want to minimize messing with them as much as possible."

"Okay. Let's look then."

The words seemed familiar, even when I couldn't make them out well. Like I'd seen them before. I was sure my mother would be better at this than me... but I didn't want to let her in on this. I wasn't sure what she would do with a new spell, or how she would feel about its future destination.

Looking at the images on the sides, I noticed one leaf seemed to be drawn in very specific detail. There were tiny sprigs in the corner as well.

"Any color on the original?"

"If there was," Willow said, "time has taken it."

"I think there are bees on this, which would indicate honey. And these look like lemons... but there seems to be an emphasis on the plant itself instead of the fruit."

Willow perked up at that. "Really?"

"Yes. I've used both a lot."

The door opened, and Lyzzie hollered, "Could use some help!"

"Be there in just a sec!" I turned to Willow, pointing to the laptop.

"Listen, is it okay for me to write on this? And mark on it? I want to see if color helps."

"Sure. Be my guest. I can make however many new copies you need."

"Come back tomorrow? You can help again."

Willow blew her bangs off her forehead, but nodded. "After classes, sure."

The door opened again, and I hurried out before Lyzzie could ask for more help. The line was out the door.

I really needed to hire more people.

Chapter 7

Willow

"Oh, sleeping beauty! Don't you have somewhere to be?"

I woke up to Tess flitting above my face. The small breeze from her wings tickled. I almost swatted at her before I realized what I was doing.

"Ugh, I've warned you not to wake me up like that. What time is it?"

"8:00 in the morning."

"It's Sunday."

"Very observant, or so you would think. But it isn't."

I should have swatted her. I pulled the blankets back over my head, trying to block out the light.

"What do you mean... oh crap, it's Monday."

I sat bolt upright, flinging the covers off me. And papers went everywhere.

"Oh, shit."

I'd fallen asleep in bed last night looking through my recipes again and working on what edits I could. Luckily, my laptop was sitting on its little desk I used, off to the side of the bed. That could have ended badly, and I really didn't want to explain it to the IT department.

Tess giggled madly and flew out the window to the garden.

I stared at the mess I had made. And then looked down at myself.

"Welp. This is grand."

An hour later, I had the floor cleaned up and papers all gathered and back in my bag. I was also out of the shower, and braiding my hair back. Tess came flying in, smiling widely.

"Is that makeup?"

"Just a little. I look like I haven't slept in a year. Leave a girl alone."

With a little flip in the air, Tess landed next to the faucet and ran her hands under the water. I eyed her, but she didn't seem like she was going to do anything evil.

"I had alarms, by the way. Why did you wake me up?"

"Your alarm went off three times. I was tired of hearing it."

"Fair." I finished my braid, checked my eye makeup, and went back to the bedroom. Grabbing my backpack, I decided I still had time to grab my first cup of coffee at the café. It was much better than what I brewed in my office and added creamer to.

When I stepped outside, I was thankful for the chunky cardigan I had grabbed. The air was chilly, colder than it had been. Winter was edging ever closer, and I growled. I loved Fall, but it never seemed to last as long anymore.

"Remember to watch the streets!" Tess said as I almost started crossing without checking.

Yep, I needed more sleep. Or coffee. Or both.

Both sounded good.

The brisk walk helped, and I made it to the café with almost no accidents. It was calm inside, as the bell jingled, announcing my approach.

"Professor! Good morning. I was beginning to wonder if you were coming today."

"Charlotte! Please, coffee."

"Always."

She turned and started making my regular coffee, and I finished making my way up to the counter. I pulled out my card and looked in the case. As she handed me the coffee, I said, "How about one of those pumpkin muffins?"

"Sure thing. That'll be $8.00."

I was fixing to reply when Winston walked through the kitchen door.

"You know, I appreciate the business, but you must spend a third of your check here."

"Ha. Ha." Then I thought about it. "Well, maybe. But it's in the budget. Coffee is very important. Then again, I didn't used to buy all the muffins."

He shook his head, loading up the display case. I took my card back, then the coffee and the ever important muffin.

Waving the coffee in lieu of my hand, I said, "I'll be back this afternoon. Later, everyone."

Walking to my office, coffee in hand, I appreciated how much hustle and bustle was still happening mid-Monday morning. It was about time for students to be switching classes, and I saw a couple of professors hurrying past me to their own courses. The coffee helped fight off the chill, and the muffin was wonderfully delicious, fluffy with a cinnamon crumble on top. I gave Tess a bit as she rode on my shoulder, huddled in the cardigan's edge and scarf I wore.

My office was chaotic as normal, but I sat down at my desk plugging my laptop into the dock and getting every-thing loaded. I finished the muffin, ignoring the work I had waiting for me. I watched Tess land on the desk. I hadn't answered emails in two days, so my inbox was probably exploding. Especially since papers had just been turned in. Many students would be panicking.

With the help of coffee, the morning passed quickly. Tess had duties in the university library and left before my class. I taught, came back and caught up on emails, chatted with a few students, and then finally taught my second class of the day. Students were indeed panicking over their paper, and I told them I was grading as quickly as I could, reminding them it hadn't even been a whole week yet.

Tess arrived at the same time I made it back to my office.

"Heading to the café with me?"

She landed on my shoulder as I made my way inside, then flew to the desk.

"Sure, why not? It's chilly outside."

I packed up my laptop and turned off the coffee pot. Putting my backpack on, I gathered the hood of my cardigan to lie on top of it, and Tess landed in the middle. I felt her sitting, pulling the hood around her.

"Good to go?"

"Yep! Thanks."

I headed out, pulling the office door closed and locking it. It was much earlier than I normally left, even on a weekday. Technically, though, my office hours were already over—I just normally liked to work here. Less distracting than at home. An image came to mind of Winston baking, and I had the thought that it was probably much less distracting than the café now, too. That said... The café was calling my name.

When I arrived at the café, the place was quiet. I grabbed my table close to the windows and Tess settled on the edge. With a coffee in hand, I went back to work. It wasn't long before Winston came out with a few things to put in the case. His shirt clung to him from the heat in the kitchen, and I bet it was very warm and cozy in there. His dark brown hair hung down into his face as he bent to put a muffin on the shelf and he caught my eye.

He had just caught me staring. Trying not to show how embarrassed I was while my cheeks grew hot, I raised the coffee cup high. He smiled, and went back into the kitchen.

I drank some of the coffee and ignored Tess, nearly rolling in laughter on the table. This was just not my day. Maybe I should cut my losses and go home. Who needed to grade, anyway? I could take a nap. Read a book. Pretend none of this mattered, and I didn't have only 16 days to finish my book.

16 days. That wasn't nearly enough time.

Or maybe it would all be fine. I had Winston, after all.

After another few luxurious drinks of my coffee, I went back to grading. As much as I wanted to work on my book, there wasn't much to do at this point until I had more information. My students would keep badgering me until I got their grades in, two week general policy for returns notwithstanding, and I wanted that off my to do list.

I was lost in grading the last few papers when suddenly, a sandwich plopped down on the table with chips and some water.

"What's that?"

"Well," Winston, who had appeared with the sandwich I now noted, said, "we call this water. It keeps us alive."

"Ha. Ha. Ha. Hilarious." I glared at him. "I didn't mean the water. I meant..." I gestured at all of it.

"This is called food. We normal humans eat it to stay alive. It might be hard for you to imagine, but there are things besides coffee."

I scoffed at him. "I'm aware. I eat food. I love food. I ate a muffin this morning."

Winston laughed, and said, "That only barely counts. And what about lunch?"

"How can you say that about your muffins? The one this morning was heaven. Pumpkin, with cinnamon swirls, and that occasional chocolate chip? It's..." I stopped, realizing that I was gushing about his own food to him, and fixing to say "orgasmic," to boot.

Foot was forward all right. Straight into my mouth.

"It's almost 4 pm. You should eat something besides straight sugar. After that, if you could help me out, I'd appreciate it. Lyzzie called in sick. I promise we'll look at the book tonight."

"We need to find you more servers. I bet I have some students who would be interested."

"Let me look at the books. And talk to my aunt. I haven't had much time to figure out all the finances, so I'm not sure of the pay I could offer."

I saluted him, picked up the sandwich, and took a giant bite. "Happy?" I said around my mouthful.

"Very." He smiled, and I almost melted right there, but he had already turned and walked back to the kitchen.

The sandwich was actually fantastic. It was chicken salad with tomato and lettuce. The bread was crispy and soft all at once. Rather yummy. Of course, it probably helped that the whole café smelled delicious.

I ate some chips and drank the water.

"I'm going to head out. Working in the café is boring. I should get back before the temperature drops anymore, anyway." Tess flew up and around me, then shot towards the front door, leaving as soon as someone opened it.

Having finished the food quickly, I packed up my notes and laptop, grabbed my bag, and headed into the kitchen. Charlotte waved as I went through the door, and I plopped my stuff on the table there.

"Charlotte is fixing to head out. Aprons are hanging up over there. I've got food to finish cooking."

"So what happens when you are too sick to work? Is there another cook?"

"Not that I know of. I have no idea what my aunt was doing."

I shrugged, curious if there'd been a magical spell she was hiding for quick cooking, and grabbed the apron. I tied it around my waist and headed out front. Charlotte was handing a customer a sandwich.

"Sorry about this."

"About what?" I asked, confused.

"You have to work?"

"You didn't call in. And besides, I'm helping in return for a favor. And maybe free coffee."

Charlotte laughed, the beads in her braids clicking. "That works. All right, it's slower usually on Mondays. Back to work blues. I'll see you around!"

She took her apron off and disappeared into the kitchen. I leaned on the counter, surveying all the food options. I'd learned how to make a few drinks the other night, but I knew there were several things I had no clue about. I'd have to bug Winston if anyone ordered them.

Charlotte was right, though, and I only had about 3 customers in the next hour. Monday afternoons were usually pretty empty. A few students were in the back corner, and mostly it was just people grabbing coffee to go.

The evening passed by, with me learning how to make 4 new drinks. Well, learned is a loose term, because Winston taught me by making the order, and I didn't have to try it.

My phone buzzed, and I pulled it out of my pocket.

Piper: Kissed him yet? -emoji-

I rolled my eyes.

Willow: No

Piper: What? Seriously? You've spent hours together!

Willow: Working in a café, mostly.

Piper: Ugh. Girl, you need better game.

Willow: I have no game Piper. What are you doing?

Piper: Ignoring my own problems. New coworker at work is driving me batty.

Willow: Ah.

The phone was silent for a few minutes, and I was starting to put it back in my pocket when it buzzed again.

Piper: Do you want to kiss him?

I felt the blush creeping up my cheeks. Too many times today, I had caught myself watching Winston as he was doing something in the café. He was so kind to every person who came in, and he remembered so many of their names. It was sweet, and they all brightened up when he talked to him.

He was certainly better at the retail thing than me.

"What has you smiling so big?" Winston's voice was right behind me.

I nearly threw my phone over the counter.

"*Don't do* that!" I exclaimed.

A few of the patrons laughed, and I shook my head. Winston just smiled like a doofus. A really hot, really fit, doofus.

"Just texting with Piper," I finally said in reply.

"Awesome. Well, we close up shop soon. I'm going to go round and talk to the couple of people left in here."

I nodded, and he went off to make the rounds and start wiping off tables. No one else came in, except for Tess. She landed on my shoulder and smirked at me. I had been watching Winston.

"Not you too." I groaned, praying she didn't say anything in earshot of Winston.

"What?" she asked, still smirking.

I shook my head and started closing down some of the less used machines. I didn't know enough to do all of them. I realized quickly that it was just Winston, Tess, and me alone in the café. I wasn't sure why that mattered now, since we'd done this twice before. But I was hyper aware of his every movement.

Tess grew bored and went off investigating in the kitchen. I wished for the thousandth time that I could fly. I'd had Tess describe it to me many times since we met five years ago. I was almost finished with my dissertation, doing a history of magic for all folks — the ones who often got overlooked in our society for whatever reason. Pixies were on the list, and she'd been the one I wound up interviewing. We'd bonded, and due to some circumstances at the time, I'd offered to let her live with me. She had ever since.

I heard humming suddenly and realized that it was Winston. He had just finished mopping up the floors and was making his way back.

"All clean?" I asked.

"Yep. Time to do so back here. Oh, wow, you've already done some. Thanks!"

"Of course. I need to learn to do more. Just in case. I cashed out the drawer, put out the closed sign, and cleaned these." I gestured to the two normal coffee pots and the two blenders.

"Hey, that's awesome. Well, if you want to learn, watch! It really isn't too difficult."

And so I spent the next 30 minutes watching Winston clean various machines. By the time he was finished, I had more of an appreciation for my coffee. Tess came by and made comments about how close we were while I tried to actively shoo her away. I felt my phone buzz a few times in my pocket, but avoided pulling it out near Winston where he might see any of the texts Piper had sent me.

Finally finished cleaning, we headed into the kitchen. I plopped down at the table. Then I looked down at my apron. The café logo was on it—a cauldron bubbling with a brown liquid—presumably coffee.

"Hey. Had a thought. You should do reward cards. Like, you get a punch for each coffee, and a free one every 20 or something."

"Aiming for freebies, huh?"

I untied my apron and thought about throwing it at him, but changed my mind. I just said, "I already get freebies! I declare it for my work."

"It isn't a bad idea. Tomorrow I've got to spend the day looking through my finances."

"Oh right. You are closed on Tuesdays. Terrible day for me to be without coffee."

"You can make your own. A whole pot. At work and home." Tess said, landing on the table and putting her hands on her hips. "I sometimes think you want to bathe in it."

Winston choked back a laugh. I shook my head.

"Okay. I have 16 days left. Less, really. I need us to get cracking. Less time spent making fun of me."

"Totally understand. I slept last night, but I started working on it. I plan to spend quite a lot of time on it tomorrow. When are you free?"

I pulled out my phone, since he was across the kitchen, and looked at my calendar.

"Class at 10 and 1. So I'm done by 3. No meetings either."

"Can you not remember your class times?"

"I can't always keep track of what meetings I have when. There are a lot of them."

"Sounds terrible."

"Nah, most are okay. All part of the job and all that. Academics is its own world, but I love it."

"I can tell. Okay, so I don't have much to give you tonight. I'm sorry. I do have this, though."

A bowl of soup was placed in front of me with grilled cheese. It was steaming hot, and the smell took me straight to fall and my childhood.

"Oh! This looks scrumptious."

Winston sat down with his own bowl. "Eat up. Thanks for the help today. And I can always make you a cup of coffee in the morning, if you're desperate."

The image of Winston bringing me coffee in bed was not safe, so I shoved it out of my mind and took a bite of soup.

Yep. Scrumptious.

I made a slight groan and heard Winston chuckle.

I looked up to see him grinning at me. I smiled back, and then quickly went back to eating.

"You are a very good cook. Did you go to school for it?"

"Nope. Just loved learning how to. My grandmother had a restaurant, and I cooked with her a lot. And with my aunt when I visited here in summer. Though we mostly baked."

"Makes sense. And potions are the same kind of thing."

"It is. Most don't really think of it that way."

"Of course it is. It is much less spooky to realize you measure ingredients and don't sing around a cauldron, hoping everyone drops dead."

Winston laughed again. "Aren't they all required to take a magical history course?"

"At our college, yes. Many of the public four-year universities require it. Though they have some choices about whether it's magical history or something else. It really depends. And of course private colleges, being religious, often don't. Those are fewer and further between, though."

"I know we did at my school. I guess I hadn't really thought about it. Of course, much of our history is a part of your history too."

"It is. But it's often a different perspective. Witches have often had to fight for their rights against a world that might not be accepting of them. I'm glad witches are still here. I cannot imagine a world without magic."

Winston made a "Hmmm" sound as he ate.

I finished my soup and grilled cheese and tried to stop lecturing. It was a bad habit of mine, even in general conversation. Hard to exit the "Teach all" mode I was in so often. I could never tell if others meant it as a compliment or complaint when people said I was always teaching them something new.

The meal finished, I sat back and examined the room. It was tidy, even though I knew Winston had been baking up a storm back here. The smell of bread was everywhere, and I wondered if a candle had been successfully made to mimic that scent. Though then I'd want to do nothing but eat bread, and that seemed like it might be a terrible idea, actually.

"What are you thinking about?"

"What?" I said, coming back down to earth.

"Your face was just so serious."

"Oh." I said, trying not to blush. "Um, nothing important."

"Come on, share." He goaded me.

"Bread." I mumbled, picking up my bowl and plate and carrying it to the sink.

"Bread? Did I hear you right?" His voice had risen an octave.

"Maybe. What if?"

"Nothing, nothing. Bread is a good subject."

I laughed, and started washing my dishes, and then grabbed his to follow, waving away his protests.

"I'm sorry we don't seem to be making much headway on this spell. I know you need the recipe."

"16 days. But it's okay. I can't force it, and you are helping me out of the goodness of your heart."

"You've covered my café now 3 times. I think I owe you."

I smiled and turned around, drying off my hands. "Agreed. I'm even having to learn to make my coffee."

"Okay. If you're done by three, why don't you stop by here? We can make some coffee and start going over what I have. If we can figure out enough, and I have the ingredients, we might even try to brew it."

"Really? That'd be amazing."

"Then maybe in 16 days, once all this is done, we could go out on an actual date?"

I stopped, having started to move back to the table. I turned to fully face him.

"Or not. Sorry. Didn't really mean to say that out loud, yet. It's no biggie. Really."

Winston tried to turn away towards the shelves. I put out a hand to stop him.

"I'm sorry," he started to back up at that reply, so I rushed on. "No, not that kind of sorry. I didn't mean to make you think I was saying no. I..."

"So you aren't saying no?" His head tilted, and he studied my face again.

"No. I mean, no, I'm not saying no. Yes. I'm saying yes."

That was the absolute most botched acceptance of a date in the history of dating. I could never tell Piper.

"Really?"

His grin nearly made me swoon. "Yes. Really." I smiled back.

And we just stood there, and I realized I was too awkward for any of this.

"Okay, so yeah. I'll see you tomorrow then?"

"Yeah, tomorrow afternoon then. I'll have the coffee ready."

I picked up my bag and slung it over my shoulder, heading for the back door.

"See you then!"

And as the door swung shut, I was met with Tess's maniacal laughter.

Shit, she'd heard the whole thing. I'd never live it down.

Chapter 8

Winston

I asked her out. Why did I ask her out? She'd just been so cute all day. And I'd seen her eying me.

And then she was thinking about bread, of all things, with that incredibly serious look on her face. How much luckier could I be as a man, to have met a hot, intelligent, kind person, interested in magic and all things witchy? Why would I not ask her out?

Because she isn't a witch.

That realization hit me as the door closed behind her, and as I heard Tess cackling at our awkwardness.

With a flick, I turned the dishwasher on and flipped off the lights. Making my way upstairs, I thought about banging my head on the wall the whole way up.

What was I thinking?

Actually, dumb question. I had been thinking about kissing her all day long. It was on my mind when I asked her out.

She just looked so very kissable.

My mother would flip. Not that my mother needed to know. I didn't want to be engaged. I wasn't engaged. She was just convinced I should be, convinced that I should agree to an arranged marriage, so I could help the Sullivan dynasty along—so I could help cement her place on the witches' council.

I did not even like the woman she wanted me to marry. Or any other eligible witch I'd been introduced to over the past three years.

My apartment was warm and quiet. I flopped down on the couch and stared at the ceiling. Now what?

With a groan, I sat up on the couch. Laundry needed to be done, and I really wanted to start work on Willow's recipe. I just needed to concentrate on it was all.

In a few minutes, I had my laundry going and a beer cracked open at the small table in the corner. I spread out some coloring pencils and the couple of pages I had. There wasn't too much to go on, but I wanted to see what I could do. First, I wanted to color everything in. Feeling the motions might help me remember something. Witchcraft and potion recipes could work in odd ways. Maybe if I drew the plants I'd be able to better read the writing.

Two hours later and I was further along than I thought I would be. The images were becoming real plants to me, but my brain was so fuzzy I didn't know which ones. Perhaps having the beer was not the best choice.

I saw Willow's face again. I'd go to sleep and start fresh in the morning. I needed to look at the store's accounts too, and call my aunt. Stumbling to the bed, I took off my pants and shirt, pulling the covers over me.

Her face was the last thing on my mind before I slipped back into dreams.

Beep. Beep. Beep. Beep.

Swearing, I batted at my nightstand, trying to turn off the alarm on my phone. I'd set it to 4 am every day, thinking it would help to keep me in a routine. That was not something I appreciated after last night. Pushing the button on my screen, I got my alarm to stop.

The blankets were warm and cozy, and I didn't want to get up yet. Plus, I had no café to open this morning. I could afford to sleep in.

Then I saw Willow's face again. It'd followed me in my dreams last night. I could use the extra time today. I had a lot to work on in a short span of time... and she'd be here at 3.

Counting to ten, I threw off my covers and stood up. The air was chilly, as I'd refused to turn on the heat yet. The cooking and baking downstairs did a lot to warm up the place anyway, so it stayed at a decent temperature. It'd got chilly last night though, and I'd soon cave.

Getting ready for the day took only about 30 minutes. I cooked an egg and some toast and sat back on my couch. I stared at my phone. What time was it where my aunt was?

The phone rang... and it was my aunt.

"You know. It's creepy when you do that."

"Ah, you always say that. I just felt I should call. What's up?"

"How well do you know Professor Willow?"

"Willow? She's grand. Addicted to coffee. So the perfect customer. Extremely kind, and quite intelligent. We had some great conversations. She sent lots of her students down to us, either to get coffee or even as employees. Oh – I should have mentioned that. You should hire some."

"She needs help with a spell and potion. She has this old recipe book she's writing a text on, and there are two of them she can't figure out. I agreed to help."

"Sounds nice of you. What does that have to do with me?"

"Oh, just, nothing really, I was just..."

"You like her."

I sighed. I couldn't ever hide anything from my aunt.

"Winston... that's a hard road sometimes. Willow loves witchcraft. That wouldn't be a problem. But your mother..."

"I know."

"For what it's worth, I like her. And as for the recipe... just be careful. We lost some things for a reason." My aunt sounded resigned.

"Mother always said some spells needed to stay hidden. We didn't really lose any, did we?"

"Your Mother would tell you absolutely not. But we can't know every spell in existence."

"Thanks for the advice. I needed to call for another reason."

"Oh?"

"Why did you have so few staff? You just told me to hire some. How did you work all the time? And what kind of pay and benefits are we talking?"

"Ah. I should have gone over all of that with you. Some of the staff quit right before I left. I figured you would want to hire their replacements. As for money, all of that is in the account books downstairs, and there are many spreadsheets. You'll make a fair amount and you can pay a fair wage with benefits, if you hire full-time. Most of the staff have always been college students, so I didn't need to worry about that. They make $15 an hour if it helps, and I let them divide the tip jar or take what's given if they are the only one working."

"Good to know. Probably should have gotten all of that information to begin with."

"Nah, you had to learn the ropes first. I'll be back in two weeks. I can stop by and help then. Toodles, dear."

"Toodles."

And she clicked off her phone. My aunt had an eerie sixth sense about things. She'd done that often in the past—contact me out of the blue when I'd needed her.

Putting my head in my hands, I took a deep breath in and out. I wasn't a lovesick teenager. We weren't even dating yet. I could figure this out. And I could handle my mother.

The table beckoned me, and so I went and worked on the recipes first. I could figure out the details for the café later.

Two hours later, I realized I had fleshed out the entire page. It was eerie how much better the spell looked to me now. I saw lemon leaves, mint bees, and rose petals. There was a spring winding in the corner of the bottom left, and a tea cup as well.

Deciphering the recipe list, I realized we would have all of this on hand. It wouldn't be as bad as I thought it would be to brew it tonight, either. There were some words I wasn't too sure about for the actual spell itself, but hopefully Willow would know those.

I stretched, reaching towards the ceiling. Feeling better about the progress on this one, I figured I could start some cookies baking downstairs and work on the other one while those baked. It was in much the same condition, but the words themselves were easier to read.

I wasn't able to get as far with it, however, even after an hour. There were so many items on the page, I wondered if it was a potion at all, or something more complicated. The timer dinged for the cookies, and so I sat it aside for the time being. I wanted to make some things for tomorrow morning, so I didn't have to worry about it tonight, and could just help Willow while she was here.

I also wanted to prepare dinner for us.

So, the rest of the afternoon whittled away, time slipping through my fingers, before the alarm went off on my phone for 3 pm. Willow was a 5-minute walk here from campus. I needed to get her coffee ready.

When Willow knocked at the door, I greeted her with a cup of steaming hot coffee. She smiled, the effect on her face nearly knocking me over. Within minutes, she was sipping it, her bag on the table, and a look of bliss on her face.

"It's perfection. Thank you,"

"I thought you might like to have some coffee after work, since you seem to have no cutoff."

"Why would I cut off coffee?" She asked.

I shook my head. "Where's Tess?"

"Out and about, since it's a little warmer today. She disappears a lot. She always knows where to find me, though. So, how did it go today?"

"Great, actually. I think I've figured out all the ingredients for the first one, but I'm not sure about the spell to go with it. The second is proving trickier, just because I'm not recognizing several of the words."

"That was the issue I was having. Let's tackle the first together. We can come back to the second."

"I'm done baking for the moment. Let's head upstairs to my table. It's comfier up there."

Willow followed, drinking her coffee and making happy sounds that did funny things to my insides. Did she know what she was doing to me? With a look at her concentration on her coffee, I'd have to say she had not a clue.

Upstairs, we entered my apartment and made our way to the table. The dinner I'd made was in the oven, staying warm, along with drinks chilling in the fridge. It wasn't a date, but I felt like I should feed her, depending on how long she stayed.

As she sat down, she dropped her jaw and stared open-mouthed at the colored sheet I laid in front of her.

"You did this?"

"Yes. What?"

"It's beautiful. Could I scan this in for my book? Would you mind? I'd give you credit."

"Of course you can. Though it's nothing special."

At that, she raised her eyebrow. I smiled.

"I like art. And I've often done similar things on other spells and potions I've worked with. It just helps soothe me, and ... I don't know. The magic works through me that way."

Willow smiled. "I always thought it was fascinating how many ways witches worked."

"My mother just yells at things and they do what she says."

"Really?" Willow looked incredulous.

"No. But it feels like it."

She laughed and shook her head.

"I understand that. Okay, so it looks like these are all simple ingredients. But the spell itself..."

Willow went silent, poring over the words, and occasionally muttering to herself as she pulled out another sheet of paper. She exclaimed a few times out loud, but if I tried to ask a question, she shushed me.

Shrugging, I prepped the food for the day. Then I turned around and just watched Willow working.

When an hour had passed, I noticed Willow shift in her attention.

"There! I think I figured it out." Willow looked up and paused.

I quickly moved over to her, acting like I'd been moving before, and not creepily watching her.

"What does it say?"

"With thine heart full and longing,
With desire, and hope twining,
Take a drink my love, my darling,
Take a drink, and see soulmates,
Love eternal, and forever,
With your heart full of passion,
Take a drink, together,
under light of full moon,
And see soulmates' desires."

She stopped and looked up. "It's a love potion?"

"Tea, more like, based on the ingredients."

"Do those... work? I'd always read they weren't very reliable? And there aren't any that I've ever seen – weren't they banned?"

"Most aren't reliable. I mean, love is a complicated human emotion that turns on the flip of a coin. Even magic cannot do everything."

"Would this work?"

I shook my head, then paused. "It... it could be possible. I know some spells were lost, or hidden, because of their power. I see nothing in this that would make it more powerful than others I have seen, but then again, I've never run across one like this. And it seems to involve both people. It isn't one to curse or trick someone into loving you."

"So what if the person isn't your soulmate?"

"Maybe nothing happens at all?"

Willow looked back down at the text and ingredients.

"Might be a bad idea for us to brew it, then."

"Why? Afraid?"

I instantly regretted every word I had spoken. I'd asked her out on a date, for Goddess' sake. Why would I ask her to drink a love potion with me?

Willow shook her head. "Not afraid. But I also don't know that I want to be aware of who my soulmate is... or isn't."

I realized she was afraid we'd drink it and discover we weren't soul mates.

I put my hands on the table. "It says light of the full moon, right?"

She nodded.

"That isn't until Friday. We couldn't do it before, anyway. Perhaps we take a break for supper, if you are hungry, and work on the 2nd spell? Then on Friday... if we decide to, we can try brewing the other one? Or both, depending."

Willow paused and looked thoughtfully towards the stove.

"It smells good in here."

"Ah, I thought I could appeal to your stomach, if nothing else."

"What is it?"

"Roast beef and vegetables. I thought I'd make something fancier than the stew."

"Yum."

After getting dinner together, I came back to a cleared off table.

"Thanks!" I sat down the plates and walked back to the fridge. "I have a bottle of red, or of Moscato in here. Or soda or beer, if you want."

"Moscato sounds amazing." Willow answered.

I grabbed two glasses and poured the wine. I sat hers down and sat across. She smiled at me and raised the glass. I did in turn, and toasted, "To Friends."

"To Friends," she echoed, and took a small sip.

"My Goddess, how is it you can cook and bake so well?"

I chucked, shaking my head. "We talked about that already."

"Yeah, but this is like excellent."

"Thanks. It's one of my favorites to cook. And simple, honestly."

"Whatever. Thanks. I appreciate the food. You keep feeding me."

"I owed you for working for hours. Call us almost even."

"Almost?" she asked, raising that one eyebrow again.

Goddess, she was hot when she did that.

"I still owe you, I think."

She shook her head and said, "Honestly, I'll take food whenever you want to cook for me."

I saw a blush creeping up her cheeks and gave her an out.

"I spoke to my aunt. She told me where the books and accounts were. I also found out I'm paying my employees $15 an hour, and two quit right before I took over."

"Ah, yes. They were fixing to graduate and wanted to concentrate on finals."

"You knew?"

"I mean, yeah. I am here like every day."

I shook my head, realizing that was more than obvious.

"Since mostly students work here, no one really gets benefits but me. I know the place makes a profit. So if I can have four employees, I would really like to hire a couple more students."

"Gotcha. I have a few freshmen I can reach out to, and they should be open to it, and that way they'll stay awhile. Only thing is that they may go home for summers."

"Makes sense. Maybe I'll get lucky. Or recruit you."

"Hey, summer is my break!"

"Free coffee?" I tried.

"Ah, I usually teach a couple of classes online anyway. I might be open to negotiations."

The rest of the dinner passed much the same. It was so easy to talk to her, and she made me laugh. If only we had more time to work on the book and spend together.

At the end of the meal, I leaned back in my chair, sipping on my second glass of wine. Willow was talking about her current group of students, and how they seemed incapable of reading directions.

"Has it not always been this bad?"

"No, it really hasn't. But there we are. I think a lot of things have led up to this being an issue. So many assume our young adults are good with technology because they've always had it — half my students weren't even aware they could take a screenshot. Sorry, here I am complaining about something that means nothing to you."

"If it means something to you, I don't mind listening."

She tipped her glass to me and drank the last of the wine.

"Wow, it's already dark outside. Time went by quickly... and I maybe shouldn't have had that much wine, what with walking home."

"I can walk you if you need."

"Oh! But you've been drinking too."

I raise my very steady hand. "I'm fine."

"Show off." She muttered under her breath.

"Listen, I love that I met you because you decided to cross the road in front of a car..."

"That is *not* why we met. We didn't even really meet then," Willow interjected.

I keep going, "But, I'd rather not worry about it tonight. Come on, I'll make us both a cup of coffee, we can talk next steps, and then I can walk you home."

Willow grumbled, but agreed. I didn't think she'd refuse coffee. She slowly gathered her backpack and purse, and we went downstairs. I grabbed our coffee and handed her a to-go mug.

"I can keep working on the second spell."

"Do you think you'll have more progress on it soon? I know you said you are working a lot."

"I have to cover for Charlotte tomorrow, so it may be a few days, but yeah, I'll get it together by Friday. And you have more than you did, right?"

"Yes. I can go ahead and start work on this chapter. Can I email you the others I have? You might have suggestions I haven't thought of."

"Sure. I can give it a skim."

"Thanks. Okay. Plans made. I'll see you tomorrow morning, then."

"Coffee, coffee. And, I'm walking you home, remember."

"Right, I..."

At that, I heard a small bell ring at the door, and we found Tess.

"It's colder than a witches' tit, no offense Winston. Can we go home now?"

"Tess? It isn't that cold yet. But yes, we are going that way. Want me to grab you something warm to drink?"

Tess buzzed in and landed on the table. "That would be wonderful."

Willow started to turn to me, but I was already pouring a bit of milk into a tiny paper cup and heating it up. I handed it to Tess, who quickly sipped it. Her wings stopped moving as rapidly as they were. "Thanks."

"Welcome. I'm walking Willow home now, if you care to join us?"

Tess gulped down the rest of the milk and flew to Willow's jacket, sitting in the hood. She gave a thumbs up. Willow shook out her hair, to where it covered Tess up a bit.

"You said pixies normally hibernate through Winter, right? Why haven't you, Tess?"

"Used too," I heard her pipe up from the hood. The walk was pretty short, which I remembered from the night I pulled her back from that idiot driver. Realizing I hadn't ever been to her home, I wasn't 100% sure which was hers.

Then, of course, she pointed to the quaintest one on the block, and I should have known. It looked like a mushroom.

"That's an interesting house," I said, examining it from the sidewalk.

"I love it. It's old too. Certainly took some fixing inside when I bought it, but I'd wanted it forever."

"It's like a fairy cottage upsized."

She laughed, "Well, I am short, so it works for me. I'd give you a tour, but I am loath to show you what it looks like at the moment. Another day, though, I promise."

"You don't keep it immaculate in case someone pops over?"

Her snort at that was probably heard down the street. "No, I usually use people coming over as the excuse to clean. Unless it's Piper."

"She seems like a good friend."

"The best. Anyway, thanks for today."

"Oh, quit babbling, you two. I'm cold." Tess yelled from the hood.

Willow looked at me for just a moment before waving and practically running inside.

Not exactly how I planned it... but then again... what was I hoping for?

Chapter 9

Willow

I walked into my house, utterly embarrassed. I felt so lame for running off... but we hadn't even gone on a date yet. The only thing I had been thinking about the entire walk home was kissing him. In front of my house. It hadn't even been a date.

I was asking him for a large favor, and sure I'd helped him out, but Goddess I felt like I was throwing myself at him. And even if he had asked me out... I wasn't sure he meant it. He'd seemed so unsure. And he hadn't even brought up it again today. He may have regretted the entire thing and decided to just not bring it back up again.

And now we were working on a love potion together.

Tess hadn't stopped cackling since we walked through the door. It was only about 6 pm, not even that late. I leaned back against the door, staring her down as she flitted above me.

"You can stop laughing at any moment, you know. It wasn't that funny."

"Uh, huh. You should have seen you two. So cute, and so very, very awkward."

I shrugged and went into my living room, dropping my bag against the couch. I was caught up on grading papers, which meant I could focus on my book, at least.

"How was your day?"

"Good. I hung out with Slate and Rose today. We worked on the gardens some."

"It's getting cold for that, isn't it?"

"Yeah. We had to go in and warm up several times. Doing it now makes it easier for next spring, and soon it'll be too cold for us to go outside at all. Rose is still probably holing up with her family for winter."

"Are you sure you don't want to?"

"What family? There's a reason I live here, remember? It's fine. I don't mind staying cooped up in this giant house versus my wee tiny hut. And, with the right help, I can always still go out with you."

I nodded, remembering the first winter we almost killed her because we didn't bundle up well enough. Pixies were so tiny that they couldn't handle the cold well, and their wings could freeze and become dangerously brittle.

Happy to have switched the subject, I kept talking about winter plans. Flopping onto the couch, I kicked off my boots and stretched out. A nap sounded amazing, but that was the wine talking more than anything. I had to work most of tomorrow. I really needed to get some work done on my book today. My agent had already emailed asking for an update today.

My phone buzzed in my pocket, and I pulled it out.

Piper: WILLOW! You have not answered me, in defiance of best friend code. I shall be there in 5 minutes.

I paused, looking at Piper's message.

I hadn't answered her?

Oh no. Oh, no. The text about whether or not I wanted to kiss him. I'd been working in the café, and hid my phone from Winston. I'd completely forgotten.

I looked around and realized I didn't care enough to hide. Piper had her own key to my house. She'd come in and find me, regardless. Sniffing out information was one of her superpowers.

I sat my laptop up on my side table, with my notes beside it as I worked on explaining the possibilities for this spell, when my door burst open.

"I'm here! Now spill your guts." Piper closed the door behind her, and I knew she was taking off her coat. Before I could say anything in reply, I saw Tess.

Tess flew straight to Piper and landed on her shoulder, and started talking. I had no doubt about who and what. I shook my head and ignored it.

"Sorry I missed your text, Piper. I was working at the café and Winston walked out right at that moment. I didn't want him to see it, so I put up my phone, and forgot."

"It's been hours!" Piper yelled, landing beside me on the couch. "I'm offended you could forget me so easily."

"There's just been a lot going on..." I tried to say, but she interrupted me.

"Oh yes, lots of time spent with Winston, I hear. Tell. Me. Every. Detail."

"Of what? I learned how to make coffees?" I replied, laughing.

"He walked you home today! He cooked you dinner! Multiple times, according to Tess. And not one kiss?"

"No. Not one."

"You want to kiss him, right? Cause if not... I mean, he is hot. I will totally try. He's even a witch."

I leveled a glare at her. "No."

"Yes! That's what I thought. Though...on that topic. You aren't a witch. Do you think he's old school?"

I sighed. "He may have asked me out... for when we are done with the book."

Piper squealed like a high schooler. "So he isn't! Or at least... not fully."

"What's that supposed to mean?"

"I mean, not every date means a man is looking for a commitment. Or woman, for that matter."

Deflating, I leaned back against the couch. "I hadn't thought of that."

"I thought you might not have. Not everyone is as serious as you."

Well, that hit close to home. I'd had a crappy relationship with a woman end badly in college, right after I'd gotten engaged to the man I thought was perfect but found out was cheating on me the entire time.

"I know the history of it, but not the science. Do witches really need to marry witches to have kids?"

Piper sighed. "By everything I've been told, witches are more likely to reproduce more witches if they marry other witches. And since there seem to be fewer witches these days... it might be true. Or it could be something completely unrelated. I haven't much kept up with the nonsense."

"I'd hate to rob him of that chance."

"A child is a child. But magic is a bond that can be hard to replace. I had a friend whose father really didn't deal well with her magic when she was a baby—her witch mother married a human without telling him. So I know it happens. I've never cared that much to look into it. I don't want kids at all."

"Your mother is still after you about that?"

"You have no idea. It's every conversation."

I shrugged. It didn't matter to me. The idea of at least one kid was always something I'd wanted, though. Could we even date, knowing that I could keep him from having magical children?

"Damn." I sighed, and leaned my head into my hands, staring at my computer.

"He asked you out."

"Yeah, but I can't even date him without having this conversation first. Goddess, we're already awkward enough."

"Tess might have mentioned that."

The aforementioned Tess finally flew over to my side and landed beside the laptop.

"Traitor." I muttered at her.

She smiled at me. "You love me. Just use the love spell thing. Then it doesn't matter."

"Excuse me, what?" Piper yelped, leaning over me to look at my screen. I pushed her back away from it.

"Chill. It looks like it's a love potion. Or tea, actually. To find your soulmate. So it wouldn't matter, now would it?"

"Unless you are!"

"Oy, Piper, what are the chances? And what if it means something completely different?"

"You know, they locked up a lot of the love and passion spells. Normal people didn't like the idea of it being used against them. Witches had to come up with a detection spell for love magic—and even then people say we could lie about it. Love is something precious, and it scares people. My mother said the only love spell she ever saw was a passion spell in disguise."

Tess sat down, her legs dangling off the couch. "It wasn't just humans. Even other magical folk, like us, and the elves, worried about it. Some say any love spell is a falsehood.

Others swore they were taken in. It was an easy scapegoat too for bad decisions, or when you were worried about repercussions."

"Are you still going to brew it?"

"What?" The change in topic threw me off. Piper was looking intensely at my screen.

"Didn't you guys say something about brewing it?"

"Um, well. He did still propose too... yeah. He's working on the other spell this week."

Piper kicked her shoes off too, and propped her feet on my coffee table. I could faintly smell her rose perfume, and wondered why she was so dressed up on a Monday evening.

"Wait a minute. Where have you been?"

"Had a date. It ended badly."

"Who this time?"

"Well, it was through one of those apps. But he freaked at me about being a witch. I swear, I may go back to the witch only app."

"I'm sorry Piper."

"It's whatever. Just frustrating. Maybe I should be more like you and date a woman."

"Do you like women?"

"There are some hot ones."

"That you want to kiss?"

Piper pulled one of my pillows to her stomach and hugged it, pouting. "Damn it, no, not really. But women seem like they'd be so much better."

"Trust me, it's all over the place there, too. You'll find someone, Piper."

"Yeah, yeah. Let's get back to the topic about your someone and a love potion."

"Thought I had you diverted there."

"Not even a chance, lady."

I chuckled a bit at that. "Thanks for the support. I do like him. He is hot, but more importantly, he's kind and smart and a superb baker. And he saved my life. He's a witch, so he won't be freaked out by what I do. And, even better, he doesn't seem to hate me for it, since I'm not a witch. Winston has been really kind about this whole thing, and just in general. Oh Goddess, plus he's an amazing cook and can make great coffee."

"You know, honestly, I'm surprised the coffee thing wasn't what you lead with."

I grabbed the pillow behind me and threw it at Piper.

"Seriously, darling, you drink so much of it. Food is good too, though?"

"Oh my Goddess, the meal he made me today was delicious. I almost asked for a to-go box."

"I always knew you could be motivated with food."

Tess kicked her feet and looked at me. "Do you like him?"

"Yes. But it might not matter if my being mortal ruins it. None of it matters right now. I have to work on this chapter. Piper? Care to add your thoughts?"

I handed her my notes, and she spent a few minutes perusing it. Tess flew off, saying she was going to nap. Nervously, I tapped my hand on the desk in front of me. Why did I feel so self-conscious about this book? Or this recipe? I'd written them before. I was published for Pete's sake! Why was I so afraid of getting this wrong?

Piper looked up at me and said, "So what happens if you guys brew this... and it works?"

She raised her eyebrows at me, and I rested my head against the back of the couch. I wanted to brew a love potion... for soulmates, with a man I was interested in.

"This is a bad idea."

"Or a very good one." She smiled. "Come on, you need someone in your love life. You've thrown yourself at your career for years. And listen, I've got nothing wrong with that, but having some fun isn't a bad idea."

"I don't do... fun. Not anymore."

"But you could!"

I shook my head. "Listen, at the very least, I guess, if we brew the potion and nothing happens, then from there it's our own choice on whether we do something, right?"

"It is. You could listen or run away. Of course, if it does something, will you be questioning your feelings the whole time?"

"I'm not scared of magic. I've done many things with various witches, including you. This wouldn't do anything but show soulmates—it's not making me fall in love with him."

"You don't know that. What if it's a side effect? Or you read something wrong. Even then, if it shows you are soulmates, will you believe it?"

"Piper... do you not want me to do it?"

"No, that's not what I'm saying. Love is a dangerous area for magic. It's why so many witches refuse to do anything with it. This one looked torn out of another book and hidden in the back, right? What was the reason?"

"The other book was lost? Messed up? It was stolen? Passed down? Who knows? Does it matter?"

Piper shook her head. "Honestly, I'm not sure. I just worry about you. And you are actually starting to like this guy. So I want to make sure you've thought this through, before you go do something you'll question afterwards."

Feeling anxious, I stood up and stretched, then walked over to the window to look outside. My front yard glittered with dew from the streetlight. I missed my flowers in the winter, but the colors on the trees were beautiful. A few leaves fell to the ground as I watched.

"I will look at it from all angles and decide Friday. I'll have a conversation with him first as well. I don't want him to feel pulled into something he doesn't want to do."

Piper came up from behind me, hugging me. "As you will, my dear."

Leaning my head against the glass was calming, as it was cold against my skin. Why couldn't things be simple?

"He may not really like me anyway, and none of this discussion matters."

"He asked you out."

"I dunno. He might have been having a break or something."

Piper pushed me into the window, and walked off, saying, "Have some confidence, chick. You are hot."

"Yeah, yeah, whatever."

I'd had enough talking about it. "What about a movie?"

We decided on watching *The Nightmare Before Christmas*, and grabbed snacks, some wine, water, and blankets, and settled down on the couch. I still worked on my book some, but it was nice to have background noise and just relax with Piper and, eventually, Tess, after her power nap.

The next day, my classes were full and ready to chatter. I made it through the first one on only one cup of coffee, grabbed quickly from Charlotte because I was running late to my office hour before class.

I deflated into my office chair, tired and ready to take a nap. Tess flapped out to the desk, landing beside my giant pile of books.

"You really should clean up in here, you know."

She picked up half the biscuit I had forgotten about, in a rush to get to class.

"Look, I've just been busy. I'll clean it up after I get the book turned in."

Tess threw her hands up in the air and flew up, spinning. "I hate to break it to you, Willow, but this is about the worst I've ever seen it. And I've lived with you for years."

Looking around, I realized she was right. My office was a right disaster, and I had students coming in 30 minutes for meetings. No naps for me.

"Okay, okay, fine. Can you get small stuff and throw it away?"

So began my cleaning, fueled by the desire to not have students think I was utterly disgusting. With Tess's help, I managed to get all the trash picked up, and most of the non-relevant books re-shelved. Grabbing the extra jacket and some cardigans I'd accidentally left, I cleared the chairs.

There. Clean. Ish. It worked.

Tess clapped just as there was a knock on the door.

"Okay, you know the drill. Out."

"Yeah, yeah. Why your school cares if I'm here or not, I have no idea. I hear everything else you do."

"Student rights. Now shoo."

I opened the door to smile at my student, and Tess took off above our heads, muttering the whole time. She was right, and I could probably have the student agree to her presence, but this had made my dean more comfortable.

Three student meetings later, I pulled out my notes for my next and last class of the day. I centered this one around the Salem Witchcraft Trials. They'd accused witches of so many things—and the real witches had shown how baseless so much of it was. I always thought it interesting that it got as far as it did. Witches had been a part of our lives for as long as history was recorded, even connected to the throne in England. That was probably part of the reason some religious group had gone bonkers against them, but it had fascinated me. It was fun to teach a whole class on it.

Tess came back in through the transom window I'd cracked above my door.

"All done?" she asked.

"Class soon. You coming?"

"Yeah, I like this one. I have to scoot after though. We've got business to take care of tonight."

I nodded, looking around the room. It felt more peaceful in here now that I had cleaned.

"Thanks for the help in here."

"No problem."

Class breezed by, and Tess went off to work. I cleaned up the rest of my office before packing and heading home. I decided to stop by for a sandwich in the café. I didn't feel like cooking, and I had too much work to do. Students had turned in a discussion board over the weekend, and though I'd put it off last night, I wanted them done sooner rather than later.

The café was lit up with the normal Einstein lights in the garden, with peaceful music seeping out through cracked windows. The windows were lit brightly, and I heard quiet chatter as I pushed open the door. Winston was standing at the counter, making coffee and speaking with the customer. I didn't see Charlotte or Lyzzie anywhere. There were five or six people in line. It was a busy night.

It dawned on me that Charlotte had asked for the night off. Winston must be on his own. Deciding on the spur of the moment, I went around the counter and into the kitchen. Winston shot me a confused look, but it cleared into a grateful smile when I came back into the café wearing an apron.

"Thank you," he muttered. His relief was easy to see, and I smiled back up at him.

"Any time. Okay, what do you need me to do?"

"Take orders? Make what you can, and I'll help till we catch up. Then I need to get some more things out."

"Done."

The next hour passed peacefully, and we worked well together behind the counter. I noticed he smelled like cinnamon and bread anytime he walked past me. Heavenly, especially when you added in watching his arms flex as he carried heavy trays.

It might be possible I was lost to this already.

Or not. Shaking my head, I tried to also shake some sense back into my brain. I could be logical about this, no matter what my apparently raging, neglected hormones thought on the topic. Winston turned, as I did, and we collided. Thankfully, neither of us were carrying anything.

His empty hands landed on my waist.

And I felt sparks fly up and down my body. Looking up, I saw his own eyes seem to gleam, the amber nearly like liquid fire.

"Sorry!" I stepped backwards, unsure of what I wanted. Or really, really sure what I had wanted, and not sure I could trust myself, to be more accurate.

"No, no, my fault. Okay, I think the rush has gone. Do you need to go home?"

I thought about all the grading I'd been determined to do. And about Winston here working alone.

"I can grade in the back? And then if you need me, I'm around? Plus, I could help close that way."

"That'd be wonderful. Wait, did you ever even get what you came in for?"

My stomach picked that moment to gurgle loudly.

Winston's smile lit up his whole face. "What do you want? I'll get it and bring it back to you. You can go set up."

Could a man say something nicer to me?

"Sandwich of some sort, and coffee?"

"Done."

"Thanks!" I said as I walked to the back. I dropped into the seat, realizing how tired I was. I didn't spend this much time on my feet in one spot normally.

Winston, wonderful Winston, brought me food and coffee. Both smelled like the best thing I'd ever had in the world. I couldn't even remember what I ate for lunch. Quite possibly, I thought, I hadn't eaten. I did that a lot when I got busy.

The next couple of hours passed smoothly as I worked on grading my students' discussion boards. Overall, I was pleased with how they did, though many were still forgetting to back up their arguments with information from the text. There was a last second rush before closing, Winston asked for my help again, and I bounced back into retail mode.

It was a nice break from the monotony of reading the same things over and over. Many of the people coming in were students looking for that last coffee to study on before the café closed. Thinking about that, I had the idea that Winston might benefit from staying open later on weekends, and certainly during the whole week of finals.

When the last customer left, Winston leaned back against the shelf of supplies and sighed dramatically.

"I never would have made it without you," he said, smiling.

"Ah, sure you would have. Most are patient. Need help cleaning up?"

"Nope. Here, take a cinnamon scone for dessert, and get out of here."

"You sure?"

I took the cinnamon scone anyway.

"Yep. Get!"

I laughed, walking through the back door and grabbing my stuff. As I left, waving and switching the sign to closed, I realized that this was certainly a life I could get used to.

Chapter 10
Winston

The café was so quiet with everyone gone. I turned on some music, letting it fill the silence. As I mopped the floors and cleaned the tables, I realized that my mind kept going back to Willow. There was just no way to get her out of my mind.

And worse, I kept remembering when we collided, and I had my hands on her hips, staring at her lips. I'd wanted nothing more than to kiss her right then and there... in front of all the customers and whoever else wanted to watch.

Damn it, this probably wasn't a good idea. I had just fled one relationship that my mother absolutely refused to let go of. If I called her, telling her I was dating... and someone who wasn't even a witch at that... She might disown me.

Did I care?

I changed the music to something poppy with more of a beat and lost myself in the cleaning. The kitchen did not take long, and I soon had all the extra items up that needed to be kept colder. Eventually, there wasn't anything else to do, so I gave up, turned off the music and went upstairs.

The apartment felt lonely. I laid back on the couch and tried to think about new recipes or items I could cook for the café. The same old sandwiches were getting boring, and I was sure the customers would appreciate some variety.

What food would Willow like?

And there I was again.

Willow surely knew about witches needing to marry other witches to more likely reproduce children with the magical gene... right? Was I insane to disregard that? Maybe. Did I care?

Not really. None of the witches I had met had snagged me so intensely. I couldn't think of anything else. Her body, her scent, her quick wit and obsession with coffee. Everything was reminding me of her. And I needed to work on that second recipe.

Groaning and rubbing my hands on my face, I sat up and stretched. Okay. Time to quit this, and do something productive. The table was piled with papers and notes. I'd glanced at the second potion and thrown things here and there last night. I hadn't concentrated on it in the least.

But Willow was counting on me. I'd spend an hour on it tonight and do more tomorrow.

The next morning dawned bright and early, and I'd barely made progress on anything. I got the café ready to go and greeted Lyzzie as she walked in. She smiled, and went straight to work, flipping the sign over promptly at 6 am.

There was always an early morning rush, with people on the way to work or school. Their names and faces were already becoming second nature, and I liked to greet them when I could..

"Winston! My man, these Danishes are fantastic. Going to have any winter specials?" Corey, one of the regular customers, asked.

"Was pondering that last night! What would you like to see?"

"Oh, I'll have to think about that. Pecan anything is my favorite. Maybe you need a suggestion jar!"

"Good thought! I'll look into it."

I smiled as he paid, leaving a nice tip, and headed out, Danish and coffee in hand.

"That's not a bad idea, actually. I mean, the pastries and stuff were always good, but your aunt has been serving the same things the whole time I've worked here."

"Really? Good to know. I'll work on looking at menu changes. Can you make a list of best sellers?"

"Yep! If you went electronic, you could track it."

I sighed, pondering what that expense would be. "I'll think about it. I'm going in the back."

Lyzzie waved her hand at me, and I started to leave - but noticed Willow walking by the window. She was bundled up this morning, with a scarf and earmuffs. The blue set off her vibrant multi-colored hair even more. Turning, I started her peppermint mocha, and threw in an extra shot of espresso. By the time she was at the counter, I was holding it out to her.

"Oh! Thanks. You know me too well."

"Nah, just predictable." Lyzzie smiled at her.

She laughed out loud at Lyzzie's response. "What's in there today?"

Pointing at the bakery display, I waved my hand. "All the normal stuff, and an apple Danish I dreamed up."

"Yum, dream food. Okay, I'll take one of those. I've got to get to class."

After she paid, and started out the door I realized I was watching her walk away in a very tight pencil skirt.

Lyzzie raised her eyebrow at me, and I sheepishly smiled, making a quick exit to the kitchen.

With several items ready to go out, I didn't need to bake or cook as much today. I decided to pour over the accounts and figure out where I stood. Three hours later, and I knew exactly why I had never liked math, and certainly hadn't wanted to be an accountant. Conversions and baking was something I just knew. All the different lines in these accounts were making my head hurt.

It boiled down to the fact that the café was certainly in the green, with plenty of money left. Having a few less employees for a couple of months had also added to what we had banked. I'd make some flyers and get them handed out for hiring someone else. As a matter of fact, I'd make one for the counter now.

Once that was done and posted, I thought about what Corey had suggested. Rummaging in the pantry gave me the knowledge that my aunt had kept everything that could possibly be of use. A jar of decent size finally appeared at the end of a shelf. I washed it out, and taped "Ideas for New Menu Items" on it, and put it out on the counter with paper and pens.

Feeling successful for the morning, I wondered if Willow would be by that afternoon. She was out on Monday at 3... Monday and Wednesdays schedules were usually the same at colleges. Of course, there was no guarantee she'd stop here.

But I still did need to ask her if she'd recommend some students to be employees...

I poked my head out the door to check on the numbers. It was lunchtime, and several customers from around the area had come in to grab something, but it wasn't too busy.

"Lyzzie? If you see Willow this afternoon and I'm not out here, can you grab me? She's supposed to recommend some students. And if you know of anyone looking for a job, send them this way!"

Lyzzie nodded and waved me off to take someone's order. The customer was an older lady who smiled broadly at me, saying "Oh, I bet my granddaughter would love working here. I'll have to send her your way."

"Thanks, ma'am. I'd appreciate it."

With a glance at the goods displayed, I decided to make a few more sandwiches. I also needed to inventory all of the supplies, and see what we had that I could play around with.

Chicken salad, cheese, different meats, and all the veggie toppings. Maybe we needed some more vegetarian sandwiches, too. That was a good idea. Or snacks. College students loved to snack. That would be a good seller when they were studying. I'd ask Lyzzie what might work later.

Three hours passed in a blur as I planned, cooked, and prepped. The clock chimed the 3:15, and I stopped, wiping my forehead. Willow might be here soon... And Charlotte would be taking over for Lyzzie. I needed to brief her on the changes.

Wrapping up my last item, I rinsed and cleaned everything quickly. I heard the door behind me open and saw Lyzzie taking off her apron.

"Told Charlotte about the idea jar and the job posting. She's excited. I'm heading out and will see you tomorrow."

I waved as Lyzzie grabbed her purse and went out the back door. Charlotte poked her head in long enough to say "afternoon" and grab her apron.

With a last look at the clock, I ducked back into the café.

There was a bit of an afternoon rush, as many like Charlotte were done with classes for the day. I helped with orders and wiping down empty tables.

Just as I thought Willow wasn't going to stop by, she appeared, smiling and radiating excitement.

"You look happy, what's up?" Charlotte asked as she went to grab her coffee.

I came around the end of the counter. She smiled broadly and said "I'm all caught up on grading. This only happens like once every four weeks, and I have more being turned in probably as we speak. But I refuse to look again until tomorrow, so I can stay with this feeling."

I laughed. "You shouldn't work off the clock anyway."

She looked around the café, then at me, and raised an eyebrow. "You are here all of the time. And I only work a few hours in the office all week. We kind of are designed to not really have a set... clock? Academics are weird."

Willow started to pay for her coffee, and I waved her off, and around the counter.

"We'll be in the back if you need me, Charlotte."

She waved us away, a smile on her face. I didn't protest the idea that was probably in her head, especially since there was another customer waiting on her.

Willow followed me into the kitchen.

She took a deep breath in as soon as we walked through the door. "I love how wonderful it always smells in here. It's even better than out in the actual café."

Her expression was so intense. I loved that she was so in love with the café and baking.

"Kitchens are their own kind of magic. I made a little headway on the second spell. Let me go grab my notes, and we can work a bit on it here."

"You sure? I don't want to keep pulling you from your job."

"Hey, I work 24/7, remember? It'll be fine."

"Eh, sorry about that," she said, twirling her coffee in her hands. "Oh, I saw the hiring flyer. I'd already emailed three students I had in mind and said you might have something up soon. I told them to drop by and just mention I sent them."

"Perfect! Thanks. I'll be right back."

I ran up the stairs, two at a time. In the apartment, I grabbed my notes and coloring pencils, and rushed back down. Willow was at the table, her laptop open, and spreading her own notes beside her. Luckily, I'd already cleaned it after my last batch of cookie dough.

"Here is what I have so far. There are a few of the names and plants I recognize. I'm worried I might have to call my mom about one or two."

Willow looked at the coloring and outlines I had done on the sheet. "Blind Eyes... that's poppy, right? And Skin of a Man... that one sounds familiar. I remember when I first started looking at the really old recipes that I was terrified."

"Yeah, that's fern leaf. They really knew how to spice up names for things back then."

"Joy of the Mountain?" Willow asked, looking up.

"That's where I hit a dead end. I'm working on the others."

"This is amazing. I can't believe I couldn't figure these out. They were just so hard to read. With your coloring and the drawings filled in... I mean, look at this compared to the original."

She pulled out another scan, and she was right. It was hard to see most of the things on the original scan. I compared them both and thought about my magical talents.

"I'm good at cooking, baking and potions, largely because I enjoy putting together the ingredients. It's something I've always been good at—and I used to color my grandmother's books. She loved to let me do it. Maybe a part of me is calling to the recipe?"

Willow smiled broadly at that. "Magic never ceases to amaze me."

I sat down with the recipe in hand. "This is for a potion, but I'm not sure what it does. I haven't deciphered any of that yet."

"Well, I can tell you that they aren't common ingredi-ents. So it may have been something the witch would have charged a lot for."

"And probably means something most people wouldn't dream of asking for. Wonder if it'll actually work. Kind of like the other spell. Many are afraid of knowing such a thing for sure."

"Piper brought that up. That most wouldn't want to actually know if they married their soulmate because they wouldn't have a choice in the matter. She thinks the spell probably does something else, and this was a nice way to phrase it."

"Not a bad point, really. Well, I can work more on this."

Willow looked at her notes and pulled up her chapter. "Well, no matter what, I knew more than I did. I need to get as much written as possible before my deadline and I have to get this to my editor. I could ask for an extension if I'm showing progress on it, I think. But we also were aiming to get these out in time for next year's classes, and we don't want to cut it too short."

"Do you use these in your own classes?"

"No, not usually. Maybe small pieces. I don't like mak-ing money off my own work, if we can support other professors and researchers, too. In the academic world, it's seen as shady if you make students buy your own book for a class you teach."

That made sense, in a roundabout way. I nodded and pulled my partly colored sheet back to me, opening the coloring pencils. Willow leaned back in her chair, folding her legs underneath her, and started looking through something on her computer.

The next hour passed slowly. I heard gentle murmurings coming from the café, and the soft jazz music playing filtered in. It was a lovely atmosphere to work in.

I also kept sneaking glances at Willow. Her multi-colored hair was coming undone from her bun, and little wisps hung about her face. Her eyes were squinted in concentration, and she was chewing on her lip as her fingers flew across the keyboard.

She was utterly captivating as she wrote.

The top and left side was filling in with various flowery shapes when Charlotte popped her head in.

"Hey boss. We're going to run low on food. The soups need stocking out here, if you can. And maybe help at the register? I haven't got to wipe down tables for a bit."

I smiled and stretched. Willow did the same.

"If you'll get the soups, I'll go help Charlotte. I need a break before I start seeing double and my fingers fall off."

"I have a potion for that."

She laughed and waved me off. Grabbing an apron, she headed out the door to join Charlotte. I heard their voices as I stood and went to grab a pot of the tomato soup to go switch with the one on the warmer. It made it easier to fill people's orders if you didn't have to go in and out all the time, and lowered the chance of knocking the chef off their feet.

We worked for an hour, taking turns doing various chores around the café. Willow manned the counter while Charlotte cleaned up and chatted with the few customers sitting around. I checked all the food and brought out a few more pastries. I double checked the dates for some, making sure none were older than a day or two – depending on the item.

"I know you are a professor, and probably a great one, but you do retail well," I said, smiling at Willow.

"People pleasing is a valuable skill in all professions," she laughed.

It'd slowed down, so Charlotte took her break.

"Dinner?" I asked Willow. "Or do you need to go? I'm sorry I keep distracting you from your home."

"No worries. Tess is out, so I'd just be watching TV and staring at my laptop. How many times can you rewatch episodes of *Friends*, anyway?"

"As many as you want, that's a great show." I replied.

She looked surprised. "I don't find many guys who like it."

"I watched it growing up. It's great."

We chatted about *Friends* for a while, before Charlotte came back waving us both off.

"Shew. Go eat. I'm sure I've got it covered until closing."

"Thanks Charlotte!" We both chimed.

"Food?" I asked, and she nodded, ducking into the kitchen. I grabbed two different sandwiches and some chips.

"Do you want Chicken Salad or turkey?" I presented the options to her once I was through the door.

She pondered for a minute, finally taking the chicken salad and chips.

We sat down next to each other at the table and started eating. After a pause, I was fixing to ask what she liked to read, when she suddenly looked up and caught me eyeing her. "What? Did I get food on me or something?"

"No. It's just... you know what, never mind. It's not important yet."

"What? Seriously, you can't do that."

She sighed dramatically. It looked like the wheels were turning in her head.

"I must know. Were they on a break?"

A laugh bubbled from my chest nearly hurting me as I heaved. She raised an eyebrow at me and waited. Slowly eating her sandwich.

"Do I get to know your opinion?"

"No. Not until you answer at least."

"Well then. I think that it easily sounded like they were... and Ross jumped the gun like a complete idiot."

She nodded. "I'll accept it."

"That was it?"

"Yep. This was delicious, thank you."

I shook my head, looking at her bewilderment. "Did I pass?"

"Yep." And her smile lit up her face. I couldn't help it. I leaned over and kissed her.

She gasped a little into my mouth, but didn't shove me away.

The flicker, the spark, I'd felt every time I'd accidentally touched her ignited. Her arms came around me, and I deepened the kiss. I couldn't get her close enough to me, and I straddled my legs on either side of her chair. As I wrapped my arms around her, she shifted, and wound up in my lap.

She gasped then, and pulled back putting her hand up to her mouth, staring at me. I don't think she even realized she'd done it.

"I... I... uh, need to go! Tess will be coming home soon."

That wasn't the reaction I'd hoped for. Well, I hadn't thought that through enough to hope for anything, actually.

"Wait, Willow, I'm sorry, I..."

She scooted off my lap, paused as if lost, then started moving again without looking at me.

"Nope, you are fine. I'll see you tomorrow."

And before I could stand, she'd grabbed her stuff, and was out the back door.

Well, fuck.

Chapter 11

Willow

He kissed me.

I hadn't imagined that, right?

Remembering the feel of his lips on mine again, I knew I hadn't. My body was on fire.

He'd *kissed* me. It had been amazing, and I'd wanted more. Remembering it made me wish I could just go back to the café and kiss him again. Thinking back to my practically throwing myself into his lap...

This was no reason to freak out. It was fine. I'd be fine. I mean, he had asked me out before this even happened. Wasn't expected, but not unwelcome. And I did think he was hot. So what if he kissed me?

Oh, no. There were so many reasons this wasn't okay.

Really though? Why wasn't it okay? What were my reasons? I mean, I had been thinking about dating him. I even almost brought up the whole "I'm not a witch, you are, could we even be together" thing... and I chickened out. I asked him about *Friends*, which I love and adore, and he even answered correctly. It was perfect.

And then he kissed me!

And oh, what a kiss it was...Which I ran away from, because I am a complete idiot.

I paused on the sidewalk, carefully looking both ways. I'd somehow made it to the street where I lived. I didn't want to cross the road without looking again. There was no Winston to save me... and I looked behind me just to check that he wasn't following me after my disastrous exit.

Seeing and hearing no cars, I hurriedly crossed the street and ran up to my front door. I unlocked it, opening it to holler, "Tess? Tess, you home?"

I heard the fluttering of her wings as she came into the living room. She flew up close to me, all six inches of her hovering in front of my face.

"Oh, you look like shit."

With a great sigh, I dropped my backpack behind my couch, and sagged back against the door as I closed it.

"Does anyone look good that close up? And thanks. Helps a lot."

"Wait... why do you look so flushed?"

"I ran home."

Tess flew even closer to my face. She looked me over carefully, and I could watch her slowly examine my every pore.

"Because?" Her voice titled up really high at the end, and she looked way too happy.

"No important reason." I pulled my phone out. I needed Piper. She'd be a great help for this.

Or would she? She might never let me live it down...

"Did you kiss?" Tess' voice nearly shattered my eardrums, her voice was so high pitched.

"Well. Maybe?"

"You did! Ooooo, call Piper! She needs to be here for this."

"Why? So you can both gloat over me? It's a weeknight. She gets up early..."

"Oh, hurry up!"

I gave up and clicked on Piper's face. Texting: News. Come over. ASAP.

Piper: OMG. OMG! OMW. FIVE MINUTES, appeared back.

Me: You live more than five minutes away.

Piper: Not today, I don't!

I could almost see the insane driving acts fixing to be committed. With nothing for it, I went back into my bedroom and grabbed pajamas. Tess followed the entire way singing "Willow and Winston sitting in a tree."

"What are you? Two?"

"K-I-S-S-I-N-G!"

Walking into my bathroom quickly, I slammed the door before she could follow. Cold water on my face felt wonderful, and I took a minute just to breathe. Then I changed, pulled on fluffy socks and my robe, and went to my kitchen. There was a bottle of Moscato in the fridge, and a bag of Colby Jack cheese squares. Perfect.

I made my way into the living room, sliding onto the couch, and setting down my treats. Realizing I'd forgotten glasses, I went back to the kitchen to grab two, and a small thing for Tess. We'd drunk from the bottle before, but I needed to watch how much I drank, or I'd be a wreck at work tomorrow. My kitchen was a mess, but I certainly wasn't dealing with it tonight.

Since I'd come back out, Tess had been flying from window to window, waiting for Piper to arrive. It was cute, but ridiculous.

"She's here!" She yelled, as I sat the glasses down. With a shake of my head, I took in a deep breath, and poured myself some wine.. I had wanted to talk to Piper, to talk this out. I wasn't sure why now I felt like I had when I'd run from the café. My pulse jumped, beating a mile a minute. Maybe because I knew I'd been an idiot, and Piper would tell me that without qualms if she agreed? Nothing like a best friend to get to the heart of the matter if you're being stupid.

Piper burst through the door, yelling, "Tell me everything!"

"Okay, but really, there just isn't that much to tell—"

"Oh, but there is something! Tell me, tell me. Now, ooo and you got wine! It's serious."

Piper, still in her work clothes, ran and sat down on the couch next to me. The front door was left standing open.

"Tess, can you get the door?"

Tess kicked it shut and flew to the back of the couch.

"Spill the beans!" She yelled.

"You guys are worse than high schoolers."

"We were lame high schoolers. I mean, really. We never got to have this much fun."

I laughed and cringed a little. It was too true. I'd been too awkward, and Piper's parents weren't very keen on the idea of her dating anyone. So we'd wound up at her house, playing games and gossiping away our high school afternoons.

"Earth to Willow? I need details. It's been a crappy day. Give me something to live for here."

Tess laughed as she piped up, "Right? I'm bored!"

"Okay! I was helping Winston in the café again today. And he made and brought me dinner. We were talking about the second potion and spell. Then I started to bring up the whole 'Maybe can't have magical children with me thing' and chickened out. I switched to asking him a stupid question, and next thing I knew..."

"He kissed you," Piper exclaimed.

"He kissed me."

"Was it paradise?"

A blush creeped up over my chest and cheeks. I could feel the heat, and just started rubbing my hands on the soft robe I was wearing to try and calm me down.

"It... it was rather nice, yeah."

"I *knew* it!" Piper clapped her hands ecstatically. Tess laughed.

"Why are you two so happy about this?"

"You need a man!" Piper said. "Or a woman, in your case, but since this is a man... you need a man!"

I shook my head and laughed. Tess flew up a bit into the air. "I mean, it may mean I eventually have to move out, or figure something else out, but you deserve someone!"

Touched, I smiled at her. "We will always work something out. I won't leave you high and dry. Hoes before bros, right?"

Tess pumped her fist in the air and yelled, "Right!"

Piper nearly choked on her wine. "Seriously?"

I giggled, and decided I needed some food in my belly. Popping a piece of cheese into my mouth, I chewed while thinking. Piper poured her own glass of wine and refilled mine a bit. After taking a sip, and feeling the bubbles go down my tongue, I ran my hand through my hair.

"None of this fixes any of the other problems. And he is doing me a favor! I can't be kissing a man doing me a favor! Plus, we have only known each other for days. *Days.*"

"Haven't you helped in the café multiple days? I don't think the favor thing counts anymore, especially not as your only contact. Don't couples write together in academics?"

Piper may have had a point. "Yes. But they are already together as a couple. And usually both academics. We aren't *together* nor is he an academic. I asked him for help. I don't want to muddy the waters."

"Oh, but it's an adorable meet cute for the whole thing. You could share it at parties. How academics brought you your soulmate! Plus, who cares about the whole academics thing. *He* kissed *you*, so it's him doing the muddying, and surely that means he doesn't care."

"I doubt we are soulmates. If those even exist."

"Done the potion yet?"

"Well, no, but –" I was cut off.

"Will you still? Do you believe in soulmates?"

I didn't know if I ever had. Maybe the idea was far-fetched. Though if even witches spoke of it... maybe there were certain people who were meant to be together...Perhaps our meeting that early in the morning, with saving my life on his first day back was a sign.

"So now what on earth do I do?"

"What do you want to do? Figure that out, and do that. I suggest going back tonight, kissing his socks off, and then making sure other clothing follows."

"Piper, that is way too... simple. And, *no* to that idea."

Tess laughed. "Yeah, and you know Willow cannot be simple. Or easy."

"Hey!" I yelled, throwing a piece of cheese at her. Piper cackled.

"It's very true," Piper added. "I mean, you might not like it... but it is true."

With a very heavy, overly dramatic sigh, I replied, "Overly simplistic, and leaves out the fact of what he wants to do."

"Oh, I think *who* he wants to do is quite clear my dear. Why do you have to overthink everything?"

"I do not!" Yes, yes I did, but I was not verbally admitting it to Piper, who would never ever forget it.

The evening devolved into fits and giggles, Piper pretending to be Winston in love with me, and Tess howling in the background. Eventually I turned on the TV and blasted the sound until I could not hear them. Piper gave in and watched a movie with me.

"While that was relaxing and fun, I've a big day tomorrow. Seriously. Try not to overthink and ruin this, okay?"

"I will attempt it. No guarantees. Now shoo. I also wanna sleep."

In no time at all, I was lying on my bed, falling asleep to the remembered feel of Winston's lips on mine.

The next morning, I actually woke up on time. That didn't always happen when I had wine. Showered and dressed, I surprised Tess when she showed up in the kitchen, already there and drinking a cup of coffee.

"Coffee?"

"Always."

"But you never make it at home." She gasped. "You aren't going to stop by the café."

"Okay, maybe I'm not ready for that, and the thought had crossed my mind I could just avoid it by making my own coffee here."

"Poor Winston."

"Look, he's a grown man. He'll be fine. I'll see him later. I'm grabbing my stuff. Are you coming with?"

"Eh, not today. It's getting chillier. I'll just hang here, since I have no work at the university."

"I'll see you this evening."

The walk to campus was brisk. There were days I re-gretted my decision to drive as little as possible. But the walk was good for me, and hopefully it would help clear my head some. The life of an academic was often pretty stationary, so I tried to challenge myself to move about during the day as much as possible.

Goddess knows my dreams last night had done ab-solutely nothing to help me. I had woken tense, and ready to kiss the first person I saw.

Shaking my head, I banished sexy thoughts from my thoughts. I had two meetings today for different committees, and I needed to keep working on my book. I had a class to teach, and also an advising appointment. It was a busy day. One I needed focus for. One I did not need to catch myself daydreaming about a certain man during.

The breeze was gentle, but chilly. The semester was quickly counting down. I looked forward to the holidays, Halloween included, and all the lights that would soon be appearing. This was one of my favorite times of the year. Leaves falling, weather changing, sweaters and boots, and hats. It was perfection.

I'd dread walking through snow later in the year when I had to, but I'd ignore that for now.

Till then, I'd revel in the times before me and enjoy every moment I could. I did hate that it was harder for Tess to enjoy it though. Maybe Winston could brew her some kind of a potion of warmth? I'd pay for one of those actually. Some days it was so cold, my toes and fingers refused to cooperate.

And there I was, thinking of Winston again. Luckily, I'd reached my office, and had to teach soon. Time to go through my notes, get ready, and look towards the day. The life of an academic was ever hectic, but I enjoyed the variety. And the students, even when driving me crazy, were worth it. The few I managed to help grow and see things differently were worth every moment of frustration.

With that in mind, the day passed quickly. I tried not to think about leaving Winston in the dark. Not stopping by for coffee when I'd done so every day. I'd even been there when they weren't open. Coffee. My coffee pot was nothing compared to the things at the Witches' Brew, and my coffee this morning, and in the office, had been lacking. I'd thought about texting him, but we'd never exchanged phone numbers since I'd been at the café so often. I could call the café... but... no.

On my way home, I seriously pondered popping into the coffee shop. We were both grown adults. We could easily handle the situation and talk it out calmly. Hell, we didn't even have to talk. There was no guarantee he'd be out front - I could even peep through the window first. Then I could just see Charlotte, grab some coffee and run.

Except, I really didn't feel like it. Not even for better coffee.

I rushed home, as the dark was beginning to set in. The wind was picking up, and I wondered if it was supposed to storm. My fingers always went numb quickly in the cold, and my jacket was starting to seriously not be enough. I'd need to dig into my closet for my heavier things soon.

Home filled me with cheer, as my solar powered lights had switched on, and little globes of light twinkled at me over my garden. I decided a fire would be just the thing, and going through my front door, I was greeted with the

TV playing another episode of *Schitt's Creek*, and Tess bundled on the couch to watch it.

"Hey, Tess." The room was a bit chilly, and not that much of an improvement over outside.

"Welcome back. Wanna watch?"

"I'll join in a minute. First, fire."

"Woohoo! Fire! I always love a good fire or two."

"Yeah, just stay away from it. Your habit of nearly giving me a heart attack because you want to fly too close is getting old." I had scary nightmares for weeks the one time Tess almost fell into the flames. I would never have made it to her on time—she'd caught herself on the grate.

I could perfectly picture Tess' wicked grin, even though I couldn't see it. Her daredevil ways were always making me worry about her.

Finally, having the fire roaring, and behind the grate, I stood up and stretched, holding my hands out to the warmth. I felt a soft thump hit my back.

"You are blocking part of the TV. Remember, I'm looking up from down here!"

I laughed, turning to find a marshmallow had hit me.

"How many of these have you eaten?" I asked.

"Hey, sugar is good for me. Now, what's for dinner? And mooove!"

With a pull, I got out of my scarf and jacket, and went to hang them up by the door. The kitchen was on the other side, so I went to look in the fridge.

"I could make some pasta. Or heat up pizza. Or... sandwiches?"

"Real chef there," Tess replied. She hadn't moved from her spot on the couch. I may have let the temperature get too low in the house for her. Looking up, I saw it was 66 on the thermostat. Not dangerous, but not the best for her. I went over and kicked on the heat, so it'd pick up the slack from the fire.

"Never said I was. Cooking has never been my thing. I think pizza."

"Pineapple and ham?"

"Always."

Turning around, I started the oven heating, and went to the bedroom to change into something comfier.

"Alright, 15 minutes, and we have dinner. Did you start this over?"

"I'd finished it again, so yeah, I'm back towards the beginning."

"I'll read a bit and watch, too. I'm tired, so I don't think my brain will have much in the way of concentration."

"Hmm, tired, huh? I don't see any coffee."

"I drank some more at work. And grabbed some from the cafeteria there."

"So you didn't stop at the Witches' Brew."

"No. It was cold. So hush."

Tess gave me a look that I knew said a thousand things I already told myself, and that she and Piper had stressed to me last night. I chose to ignore all three of us as a group, and picked up my book from the side table.

Time for some dragons, romance, and less real-life drama. That sounded fantastic to me.

I read, occasionally get distracted by scenes in the show, or Tess laughing merrily at something said on the screen. This was one of her favorite things to do in the winter, and I was pretty sure by this point she could act out this and several other shows as a one-person act, line for line. I tried to get her to read some, but she said it just wasn't her style.

The oven dinged, right as the characters in my novel kissed for the first time, and I don't think anything has ever had better timing. I'd already been imagining them as Winston and I. Not good.

"Earth to Willow—Pizza?"

"Yeah, yeah. I'm going."

"Good scene?" Tess asked while trying to look at the page I was on. She loved to sneak up behind me and read the spicier scenes aloud.

"No." I slapped the book closed and sat it on the table. My blanket took most of my warmth with it, and I wished I'd had the ability to just zap the pizza to me. Or levitate it out of the oven. With neither of those choices available to me, I went to get it out, so it'd stop cooking in the still hot oven—even if it did switch off.

I chopped up half of the pizza in normal slices, then took a slice and cut it into rather small squares for Tess. Putting ranch into two dipping bowls, I dropped the plates onto the coffee table.

"Heavenly." I said, as I smelled the sweet pineapple and all that bread. Divine creations, no matter what anyone argued.

"The best." Tess agreed. We ate while watching the show, and I began to look towards tomorrow. Would I still avoid the café?

I couldn't. Tomorrow was Friday. The night of potion brewing. I could avoid it in the morning though....

That seemed like a much better idea, really.

Yep. I'd make my own coffee in the morning.

Chapter 12

Winston

"Stupid, blasted, idiotic, thing." I slammed the door shut, ready to throw everything on the cookie sheet in the trash.

Charlotte poked her head in, concern written all over her face.

"Boss? You okay?"

"What?" I almost snapped, but was confused. Then I realized I was standing there screaming at the oven and probably looked like a maniac.

"I... Yes. I'm fine. I just burned something."

"You've never burned anything since you got here. You sure you don't need a break? We have enough..."

A break would give me time to think. And I didn't want to think... It always led back to...

"No. I'm good. Just let me know if you need help out there."

"I mean, honestly, when you were in here this morning, and looking like you might rip someone's head off if they moved wrong, I think you scared off more people than helped... Maybe just stay back here and make more cookies?"

She popped back into the café before I could come up with an excuse.

The cookie sheet was still hot, so I set it on top of the oven after dumping the burnt to a crisp cookies into the trash. An entire batch wasted. I'd never burned food before. What was wrong with me?

And then I remembered why I'd been in such a foul mood this morning. Willow hadn't come by today. And though I kept waiting for her she hadn't shown up yet. So, I kept waiting, like a lovesick puppy for her to show.

I was not that pathetic. I didn't need to know what had happened. Clearly, the kiss had scared her off. Or landing in my lap, maybe. She wanted nothing to do with me like that. Fine. That was fine. She'd said it was okay, but I hadn't heard from her since.

Tomorrow was Friday though, and the full moon, and we had a love potion to brew together of all things. How on Goddess' Earth did I manage to get into such situations?

Gathering ingredients again, I tried to lose myself in the baking. An hour later, I had peppermint mocha cookies that were to die for, and that did not by any means remind me of Willow. Or hopefully magically call to her with her favorite things.

If I could make cookies like that... Was that possible? So much of potion making was ingredients and intent. I'd certainly seen potions put in things... So perhaps it wasn't far off the mark. A thing to explore in the future.

For now, I had cookies... and no one to talk to.

My phone rang in my pocket, and Brian's face, so like mine, popped up on the screen. I answered.

"Hey! What's up?"

"Man, what's eating you? I just got a text from our aunt to call you."

"Figures. Why didn't she call?"

"Who knows? Probably partying. Anyway, no changing the subject on me. Dish."

I sat heavily on one of the kitchen chairs, surveying the disaster I had left in my wake. It was going to take a while to clean all of this up.

"Dude? Seriously?"

"Sorry, sorry. I... kissed someone." I heard the tremor in my voice, and laid my forehead down onto the table.

"Oooo, nice. She hot?"

"That's your first question?" My voice dripped annoyance. My brother, always asking the important questions.

"Well, duh."

"Yes. She's hot." That was easy enough to answer.

"So, what's the problem?"

"She ran out and I haven't seen her since then? I mean, it was only yesterday, but..."

"Ouch. That is a bit of a problem. Did you call?" His voice sounded reassuring, and I was glad he had called, even if I didn't really want to talk about it.

"No. I... she comes by the café like routine. When she didn't show after... well I figured that was a message in and of itself. That, and I may not have her number. She was always here. We just hadn't exchanged them."

"Okay, so no biggie. Maybe she just needs to process, right?"

"Maybe. We have a thing scheduled tomorrow evening. Maybe she is just waiting to talk."

"Exactly it. Don't lose all hope. Besides, you've been there like what, less than a month? How well can you know her?"

"It feels like forever. And we spark when we touch."

"Romantic." I could hear the laughter in his voice.

"No, like, I literally feel an electric jolt."

"She a witch?" And that question brought it all home.

"That is the difficult part."

"Mom's gonna flip on you, dude." I could hear his voice get a bit higher. He knew the pressure she put on me.

"Couldn't you have taken longer to get married?" I whined. "Now Mom spends all her energy on matchmaking me instead of the both of us."

"Sorry man, Jill was perfect, it's just a bonus she's a witch. Though we had a rocky start, too. Listen, if you like the girl, go for it. Mom can get over it. And marrying someone you do not love is miserable, if mom and dad are any indication."

"Ha. Yeah."

"So, I say go for it. Pull out all the stops. Win her over." He sounded excited at the prospect. I would have, before that kiss.

"Don't you even want to know anything else?"

"You like her. You have good taste. That seems enough. I'm sorry, do you wanna gush over her?"

I heard Jill holler in the background, and my brother laughed. "Jill agrees, because she wants to hear it. Putting you on speakerphone."

"Hey, I didn't agree with any of this."

Jill apparently joined the call, asking, "Please? Come on, I need something in this life besides the baby."

I laugh, and decide what the hell. "Her name is Willow. She's a professor at the university here. Teaches History of Magic."

"And she's not a witch?"

"Nope. Just always loved it. Her best friend is a witch. She also has a coffee addiction, loves peppermint, and thinks bread is the best smell on earth."

"That's cool. You two might just be meant for each other." My brother sounded sarcastic.

Jill retorted, "Oh shut it! She sounds wonderful. So she likes the café?"

"Yep. She came in all the time and also talked to Aunt Maggie, so she knew it well."

"I hope you two work it out. You sound like you respect her, and like her. That's important."

"R-E-S-P-" my brother started, before I heard Jill wallop him one. Then a baby cried, and Jill sighed. "Thanks for the break," and I heard her take off.

"You forgot the description part, though."

"What do you mean?" My brother could be annoying as hell sometimes, but he'd managed to make me feel less crappy.

"What's she look like?"

I laughed, "Shorter side, hair dyed bright multi-colored. Dresses in a lot of black, but mostly professional clothes for work that honestly... do great things for her figure."

"Nice. I can't wait to see a picture. Okay. Let me know how it goes, yeah?"

"Yeah. Thanks."

"Anytime. We'll have to come visit soon. Laters!"

I was alone again in the kitchen. But suddenly, it didn't seem too awful anymore.

Over the next couple of hours, I constantly pulled my phone out multiple times, trying to decide whether I wanted to try and find Willow's number. Honestly, Charlotte or Lyzzie or my aunt probably had it... Or I could find her on socials. Or her school email...

Could I just send a message asking if we were on for tomorrow?

Would she respond? Would it be unfair to place that one her? I needed to know though. There were things to set up and ingredients to gather.

Even with my brother's encouragement, I worried about whether this was a good choice. My mother would be furious. Did I care? I wasn't sure. At some point, it would probably upset me, but overall, it was my life.

My mother had tried for years to get me to marry a woman of her choosing. A witch of her choosing. And even the witches I had met myself and dated had never enchanted me the way that Willow had.

I deserved to be happy, even if it meant that I wouldn't continue the Sullivan line. Maybe witches were meant to decline. Maybe the magic was changing. As long as those we married were okay with who and what we were, it shouldn't matter who we fell in love with.

I nearly dropped the dish I was washing back into the water.

Love? Had I just thought love? Did I love her?

Maybe. I didn't know her well enough to decide that yet.

What did it matter if she ran away when kissed?

I could text her....

Lyzzie poked her head into the kitchen. "Hey boss. It's pretty slow in here. Why don't you take a break?"

I raised an eyebrow at her. "Why are you guys telling me to take breaks now?"

"Honestly? Charlotte and I decided you need pushing and taking care. You hardly ever stop to eat. So go take a walk and eat something. It'll be fine in here."

I stored the dishes and drained the sink. Everything was caught up. The university was close by. It was after 3 pm, so Willow would probably be home. I wouldn't run into her there.

With that plan in mind, I packed a sandwich and chips, and bundled up in a jacket and scarf. I waved to Lyzzie and headed out. The wind from yesterday had gone, leaving leaves scattered everywhere.

Though I used to visit as a kid, the place looked different these days. The campus was the same old brick buildings, towering over the rest of the neighborhood which consisted of Victorian homes, owned by professors or rentals for students. Lights hung around campus, twinkling in the dusk light. Atmospherically, it was easy to fall in love with, so magical.

The campus map showed several buildings, each named after someone in the key below. Probably someone who had donated a lot of money, or helped create the new school or department. Typical. I decided to walk around instead of going to any one building.

Finding a statue of a fairy with her wings furled out, hovering over a unicorn, I stood looking up at it. The stone seemed to shimmer in the light. It made me feel free, looking at it. There were so many magical creatures and people in the world.

A picnic bench sat nearby with no one at it, so I went over and sat down. I pulled out my sandwich and ate, breathing in the fall air. The campus was alive at this hour, with the sounds of students laughing and music playing in the distance.

During warmer days, I wondered how many students stayed out and about, studying in the sun. There was something to be said for college life. When you could study, learn, and party, with so fewer cares and fears in the world. At least, for some students, this must be the time of their life.

I looked at the statue again, wondering at what life had brought. Witches had always been in the open, even during the attacks that should have driven us off. Luckily, people had wanted the magic more than they had feared us. Some creatures had not been so lucky.

The sculptor had captured the unicorn so realistically; I felt as if it would move at any moment.

Unicorns had been hunted to near extinction, because people–including witches–had wanted their horns. Elves had stepped in, taking the remaining unicorns to their vast forests and hiding them behind their own protections.

I'd seen a unicorn once at a sanctuary run by Elves in California. It had been beautiful—shining white, with a glow that made you feel as if you had never known true majesty.

As for faeries—I'd met a few. Many of them also lived with the elves. They did not like technology. Said it messed with their ability to speak with nature. And so they retreated from the world as it became more and more modern. The natural parks and other sanctuaries had given them a way to stay true to who they were.

It didn't matter how public we were, all non-humans and those gifted with magic alike. Normal humans outnumbered us in all our iterations. Magic had to fight to stay in this world. We had to fight to stay protected. And in every century there seemed to be a group that wanted to blame us or take us out as their scapegoats.

An hour later, I decided it was time to head back to the café. I felt refreshed and excited. There had been perhaps too many days spent at the café without leaving. Besides, I had interviews to get to.

The fresh air had done my brain some good—and given me a chance to think about other things. I had another spell I could work on in the meantime, between today and tomorrow afternoon. I could work on that and concentrate on being ready. If Willow showed, she showed. If not, I had all the answers I needed.

There was no line when I got back to the café, and Lyzzie smiled broadly at me.

"Better?"

"Better. Thanks. Has W...." And I cut myself off.

Lyzzie knew, though, and shook her head. "The first interviewee is here though."

I went behind the counter, checking to see that we had enough pastries and other things needed for the rest of the evening. It looked stocked, and a full coffee pot waited for those who needed it. A few students sat around tables chatting, and I spotted at least one other professor I had met.

I should rename The Witches' Brew for something more academic. We sure attracted them all. I was even interviewing students. Speaking of...

"Lyzzie? Which one is it?"

She waved at someone, a chipper looking dude, and he came over. That start a string of four interviews that mostly went well.

Relaxing again, I went back into my kitchen and then up to my apartment. Lyzzie could holler at me if she needed me, and I didn't need to hang out in the kitchen to make anything. The dining table awaited me, the spell sitting where I had left it.

Grabbing my coloring pencils and laptop, I once again sat down to figure out what I needed to know. What was the spell, and what were the ingredients?

Time passed, and I still wasn't sure I had accomplished anything. Some names I had thought I had traced seemed foreign to me. My mother might know better what I was looking at. I could call her... but I really didn't want to. There was no way I'd listen to another lecture from her.

Then again, she might be what I needed to figure this out for Willow, and it'd be easier now than later when she knew about that.

Before I tackled that, though, I needed to check on the café. Stretching, I leaned against the wall, and counted, feeling my back burn from sitting still for so long. The café was still quiet, and Lyzzie told me to quit worrying.

"You know, we hardly saw your aunt. Food appeared, we sold it, and off we went."

"Yeah, but there were more of you."

"Ah, Charlotte and I were the most talented. You are working on hiring someone else, right? It'll be fine."

"Two someones, at least. And thanks. How much longer till you graduate?"

"You've got Charlotte and I both for another year."

"Perfect. Okay, remind me to have you train your replacements too, before you leave."

Lyzzie laughed, and I went back into the kitchen. I already fixed much of what we needed in the morning and it was ready to go out. I didn't need to bake anything. It was still a couple hours till closing, too.

Time to face the music, and call my mother.

Upstairs in the apartment, I found myself trying to push it off again. I grabbed something for dinner, started laundry, and kept trying to find small tasks to distract myself. When at last I'd exhausted every possibility, I gave up and fell back onto the couch.

I could just scroll on my phone instead...

And that's when it rang.

Mother.

Had my brother said something to her?

"Hello?"

"Winston? I haven't heard from you in days, and your brother just mentioned you. Are you okay?"

Of course he had. I owed him now.

"I'm fine, mother, really. You?"

"Doing great! The museum is doing well. We are getting in a few new pieces today."

"Sounds great. Hey—speaking of pieces. A friend of mine found some old spells in the back of a book. Looked like they were stitched into a new grimoire instead of copied. She was having trouble figuring out one of them and asked for my help."

"A witch, hmm? Maybe it isn't wasted that you moved down there. Why your help?"

I decided, after keeping myself from correcting her, that it'd be easier to pretend I hadn't heard her assumption.

"We ran into each other. She comes to the café a lot. She's a professor at the university here and was writing a book on them. Has a deadline, and was worried about meeting it."

"Academic witches are such an odd bunch. Of all the ones you had to pick, an academic doesn't seem like it'd suit you."

"Anyway," I said, avoiding that landmine, "do you think you could help me figure out a couple of these? I didn't really mess with old ingredients at all. I usually learned by following someone else doing the spell. I didn't read many recipes."

"Much of spell making is taught by oral tradition, and by simply showing someone younger than you. That practice could also help keep precious spells used to make money in the family. You say she's working on a book?"

"Yes. It's some history of magic and witches, common spells, and the like. Plus, this book she found."

"Some spells are better left forgotten. What is it for?"

"I don't even know. I can't get that far."

"Fine. Tell me some names then."

I could hear the annoyance in her voice. But I wasn't being yelled at, or given the silent treatment, so there was that.

"So first there is Skin of Man. Then Semen of Hermes. I figured out that Blind Eyes was supposed to be Poppy."

"Well, the first is easy. That's Fern Leaf for Skin of Man, and the second is dill. As to the third... I'm not sure. I'd say consult your aunt."

"That helps. Are you sure about the first two?"

"Positively."

I made several notes and rubbed my forehead. If that was the case, I needed to look up pictures of these and compare them to what I had drawn. I wondered if fern leaf in a spell ready capacity was easy to get or not.

"Thanks mom."

"Those are strange combinations. When you figure it out, let me know. Perhaps this spell was lost for a reason."

"Yeah, yeah. You guys made several go away. What's the harm in sharing a spell? It's in a textbook, anyway. Mostly only students will read it."

"Not so. It's a good way to get several new spells, or try out other versions of your own. And there are many reasons to not share everything. We banned love spells because they are extremely tricky and can have dire consequences. Same with ones to induce passion, or hatred. Curses should never be shared."

"People can always try to make their own."

"True, and I'm sure they do. But no reason to make it easy for them."

"Okay. I'll let you know if I figure out the potion and the spell. If you figure out that third ingredient before hearing from me, call or text it, please."

"Of course. I..."

Lyzzie hollered up from downstairs, "Winston? I'm almost done closing and fixing to head out!"

"Oh, I'll be there in a minute!"

I stood up, stretching as I did so. I'd been at this a lot longer than I had meant to be. "Sorry mom, gotta go. The café is closing."

"You have to be there for that?"

"Yes, mom. Night. And thanks."

"Hmmm, just wait. And I want to hear more about this girl."

"Night, mom. Love you."

As soon as she replied with "Love you," I hung up. Otherwise, she'd keep bringing up something else. I stuck my phone in my pocket and hurried downstairs. Lyzzie was hanging up her apron.

"Hey! It's all set. You didn't have to come down."

"Ah, but I enjoy making sure everything is okay. Plus, I need to check stock for tomorrow. Sorry, did we get busy? I meant to come back down earlier and check on you."

Shrugging on her jacket, Lyzzie shook her head. Bright red hair fell into her face, which she pushed back as she wound a scarf around her neck. "It was fine. Thursdays normally are slower. I think there was quite a bit in the pastry case, so I wouldn't sweat it too much. I'll see you tomorrow evening."

"See you then!"

Lyzzie went out the back door, and I locked it behind her.

Time to bake some cares away, and keep working on that spell.

Chapter 13
Willow

The morning dawned bright and way too early. I threw my pillow at the window, wishing I'd remembered to close the curtains. Why did I always try to leave windows open for Tess?

I should have kept the pillow to put over my head. Awake and aggravated, I sat up and stretched a bit. It was not even 7 am.

"Coffee. Java. Caffeine. I need it."

"Are you going to make your own?"

I glared at Tess, who flew in looking wide awake from the living room. She was dressed in a long sweater and tights, rocking bright neon colors. She practically glowed as she flew.

"Goodness, you look cheerful. Stop it."

"Ha. Ha. I lost a bet. Okay, let's get ready to go!"

"Let's? Are you going?"

"Of course. I wouldn't miss today for the world. Come on, up, up. You're doing a love spell tonight. You gotta dress the part."

And then I heard my door open. Piper rushed into the bedroom, looking bright eyed and way too chipper for this early in the morning.

"What is wrong with all of you?" I asked. I tried to lie back down and throw the covers over my eyes.

"Oh, no you don't. I brought doughnuts. And one small cup of coffee."

I smelled the aroma, and sat back up. Piper was waving it close to my face. I glared at her. She just smiled and handed it to me.

With a deep drink, I decided I forgave her. "What on Goddess' green earth are you doing here?"

"Big day today. And after the runaway kiss?"

"You named it?"

"Too easy not to. Now, you need to look like you aren't the witch drug in after nearly being burned at the stake. Sip on the coffee, and get in the shower. Go, go, go. I'll work on outfits."

"No, no, you won't. I don't trust you. I have to work today too, you know."

"Yes, yes. Now *go*."

Piper pulled the covers off the bed, effectively stealing all my heat, and pulled me into the shower. I continued drinking the elixir of life, and glaring at Tess and Piper as they grinned wickedly, pushed me in the bathroom, and shut the door in my face.

I didn't even have clean underwear to change into.

There was no help for it. I grabbed a towel and threw it on the rack by the bathtub. With a few more gulps, I finished the coffee, turned on the fan, and hopped into the shower. The heat did wonderful things for my brain and helped to wake me up.

I was toweling off when the door opened again, and Piper stood there with a light gleaming in her eyes.

"I'm fixing your hair."

"What? No. I'm putting it up like I always do for teaching."

"That tragic bun? Or down? It never lasts, you know. Come on, let me curl it a little and create a nice up do. You'll love it. And you have time before you have to teach, right?"

"Yes." Darn best friends, memorizing your schedule. "Don't you have to be at work?"

"Nope, flexed an hour. Okay, come on, come on. Here is a bra and underwear I grabbed out of your dresser. I'll leave you alone for a minute, and then you can pick your outfit. I have three choices."

Three. Choices.

"It's not even a date!" I yelled towards my bedroom. Mad cackling echoed back to me.

Really, I should have seen this coming. The underwear I was holding was lacy, and I couldn't even remember buying it or the bra. It was sexy looking and did good things for my figure. With the towel wrapped around my hair, I stepped out, half scared of what I would find.

And realizing that my heart was beating a little too fast.

"Okay, so you have three options. You have these nice wide black dress pants that would go lovely with this dark purple sweater. It's nice, but low cut. Professional and sexy. I love it. Took the liberty of finding some matching jewelry."

Tess flew over the second option. "Pick this one! I chose it."

"The second option is this flowing black skirt, with this starry top of yours. Also, low cut. The skirt, as I'm sure you know, fits your bottom quite well."

"I... well. Yes. I don't normally wear it when teaching."

"Everything should hug one's butt. So what does it matter?"

I glared at her and crossed my arms over my chest. I felt even more exposed.

"Okay, option three is my favorite. It's this dark blue sweater dress, and gold and navy starry tights I found. I think with these black boots, you'll look amazing. It's also comfy looking, and therefore easy to work in."

I stared at the three options, wishing for another coffee.

"It's not a date."

"Nope, of course not. You are still wearing clothes, though, right? I mean, if not, I can look into some other options..."

"Yes! Clothes. I am working first."

"Ooh, but maybe later no clothes? Nice distinction. I chose your undergarments with that in mind."

By this point, my head was in my hands, and I was hoping the rest of the day would be less chaotic. Of course, I knew what my day held, so that was likely not the case.

"I like option one. Those pants are comfy. Could I not wear the star top with it?"

Tess flew back and forth and then nodded. So I grabbed those and tried them on. The pants were wide legged, but hugged my body. They were also soft, and I liked to wear them often because professional meets comfy is always a win. Though, usually I'd choose a more casual top.

"You could go to a funeral in that." Piper said, looking at my mostly all black ensemble.

"I wear all black all the time. And this shirt has a lot of gold on it."

"Sure, sure. Okay, let's get your hair fixed, shall we? Oh and jewelry. Hmm, let's still go with these."

She held out my gold dangling moon and star earrings, and my gold star necklace.

"Not too on point?" I asked with my eyebrows raised.

"I've seen you wear this together at least ten times. It's pretty. And I pulled the gold moon clip for your hair. Come on."

Impatient as ever, Piper pulled me in front of the mirror and grabbed a chair for me to sit on. Then somehow a bag appeared, from which she pulled a curling iron, a straightener, and three or four bottles of who knows what.

"I have some of these things you know," I said, gesturing to the tools.

"Mine are better. Okay, so tell me how you're going to handle seeing him after avoiding him so well."

I winced as Piper blew my hair dry. I hoped it didn't frizz up, but then noticed she was also massaging some kind of liquid into it. It felt amazing. We should have spa days more often.

"I was going to go in for coffee, say hi, and um, ask if we were still doing the thing tonight, and ask to talk?"

"Very adulty."

I could hear the sarcasm in her voice.

"What, should I walk up and ask to talk about how I ran from the room after he kissed me?"

She snorted. Tess laughed.

"Oh, or maybe I should just run up to him, jump on him, and kiss him?"

"Now, I like that option." Tess said, laughing.

I couldn't move my head, or I'd glare in her direction.

"It's not a bad idea. I mean, he kissed you once." Piper added in.

"It'll be in the café in the morning. Way busy. Nope, not happening."

"So people are the only thing keeping you from kissing him again?"

"Look, I'm not saying I don't want to kiss him. I just think there is a lot we need to discuss before we go down that road again."

"Go in for coffee, apologize, make plans for this evening. Call me immediately and tell me all of it. Go to work, do the boring stuff, and then head to the café. Text me when you are on your way. And then, do the spell and the talking. Immediately call me the second you are on your way home."

"Okay, okay, okay. I will let you know how it goes."

"If I don't hear from you, I'll know that you are just having a great chat."

I could see Piper in the mirror in front of me, gleefully smiling.

I groaned.

"Or she could call you and leave it on speakerphone? Or maybe I'll hide somewhere and watch."

"Tess, you absolutely will not. I will leave you here today if you can't behave."

I felt fidgety and just wanted to get up and walk in circles. But Piper was dutifully curling my hair and setting it down so carefully.

"I can't believe I let you do this."

"You'll thank me when you aren't wearing a tired t-shirt bra later."

Twenty minutes later, I was fully in makeup, my hair done in some braids, and curls, and dressed to the nines. I put on my nice jacket, with a sherpa hood, and Tess curled up inside it.

"You are all insane."

"Go, go," Piper said, following me out of the house. She took off towards her car, and after hefting my backpack up on my shoulders, I headed towards the café.

"Could just skip the coffee." I muttered under my breath.

Tess' voice piped up from my hood, "Don't you even dare think about it!"

"Okay, okay," I grumbled.

Before long, the café and all its gentle noises appeared. I rounded the corner and paused. I could do this. I was a grown woman. It was just a kiss. This would be easy. Right?

The voice in my head was trying so very hard to convince me otherwise.

Shrugging my shoulders, I went to the door and paused again. It felt as if my shoes were stuck on the sidewalk. Then the door opened, and I nearly got clocked by it.

"Sorry!" the person said as they hurried off, worriedly clutching their coffee. At least I wasn't wearing it.

All right, that's it. I grabbed the door before it swung shut and entered. The smell of coffee and bread was more entrancing than it should have been. I breathed deeply and let it bolster me.

Winston stood there, staring at me. His gorgeous eyes seemed to drink me in, and I could see a hurt there that wasn't before.

I'd done that to him. I'd been too scared to see him, and I'd hurt us both.

Charlotte was standing at the counter, and she waved at my face.

"Earth to Willow. You're next!"

Connection broken, Winston turned back to the coffee machine. She had already rung up my coffee.

"Pastry today? There are some new chocolate muffins with peppermint chips."

"What?"

I looked down into the case to see magnificently huge chocolate muffins with little red and white chips in them. Looking up, I saw Winston smiling at me.

"Yeah, I'll take one."

"On the house," Winston said to Charlotte. I paid for my coffee and took it and the muffin.

"Hey, um, can we talk really quick?"

I said it so quietly, I wasn't sure he'd heard me. He nodded, though, and motioned to the kitchen door.

"You okay for a minute, Charlotte?"

"More than, boss."

Her smile was huge, and she winked at me.

What on earth?

I followed Winston, not having time to investigate it. He went into the kitchen and stood awkwardly with his hands in his pockets.

I was holding a muffin I desperately wanted to take a bite out of, and my coffee. I took a sip as the door swung shut behind me.

He just waited, looking at me. Yeah, I deserved that.

"I'm sorry," I blurted out, right as he started to say the same.

I waved my muffin at him. "No, don't talk. Look, there were things I wanted to discuss with you, and even then, I shouldn't have just run off and avoided you because you kissed me. We are both adults. I assume we could have handled it. I should have... I should have just talked to you."

"You *were* avoiding me then." He said, sad.

"I haven't had a great track record in the relationship world. And like I said, I wanted to talk about some things. So. Tonight? Are we on for the potion? And then we can talk?"

There was a pause as Winston looked at me. I took a giant bite out of the muffin.

It was absolutely delicious, though, and Winston choked back a laugh.

"Do you like it?" he asked, the spark returning to his eyes.

I managed just to nod, as I had to keep chewing.

"It was inspired by you."

I felt my eyes open wide, thinking of what that meant. He'd been thinking about me. So much so that he had *baked* something just for me.

"And yes. I already prepped for the potion. It has to be done under the moon though, so I think we can meet and talk beforehand. Maybe dinner?"

I nodded, swallowing my bite of muffin.

"That sounds great. I'll be here around 3? Or is that too early?"

"Should be fine. Lyzzie's set for tonight. I'll see you then."

I nodded and went out the back door.

"You were uncharacteristically quiet," I said to Tess. I pinched off a bit of my muffin and handed it to her.

"I thought it'd be unfair for him to know he had an audience."

I laughed a little and nodded. "Might have made it worse. All right, let's get to campus, and I'll message Piper."

Piper's resounding reply was to scream text "He made muffins for you" at me with about a hundred exclamation points. After that, all sense was gone. I got to work, grading and teaching. Fridays were lighter usually, and I didn't have any meetings.

When 3 pm rolled around, I had to convince myself to leave campus. I could have gone home first, but Piper had already put so much effort into my outfit and hair. No sense in changing now.

I looked up at what time the moon would rise. Around 8 pm, which meant we'd be together for 5 hours before we began performing the spell—though I wasn't sure how long it would take to make the potion.

Still, even that late... that was hours together. What if the conversation went horribly? What if he decided he wanted nothing to do with me? What if the fact that I might not produce magical children would make him regret his choice?

Tess joined me as I headed towards the café. It'd warmed up, but she still huddled in my hood.

"Do you want to go home?"

"Not really. I'm curious about tonight. I can be there in case neither of you remembers what happens."

"I don't think that's likely."

"Ah, still. I'll hang out in the café for the rest of it if you want me to."

"I'd prefer that, yeah."

I heard her mumble, but knew she'd listen. The walk to the café wasn't far, and I stood outside for a few minutes once again, waiting to see if I would panic. Charlotte waved to me on her way out, and I waved back. I remembered that grin from earlier and almost asked her about it, but chickened out.

Inside, the café was warm, and smelled great as usual. Tess left and flew off to do whatever she had planned. I waved to Lyzzie, who was also grinning, and went into the back kitchen. Winston was nowhere to be seen, so I went upstairs and knocked on his apartment door.

He opened it, apologizing. "Sorry, sorry. Lost track of time working on this. Come in, come in."

The table was strewn with papers and coloring implements. I dropped my bag on the couch.

"What are you doing?"

"I had quite a few pieces of this second one worked out, but I'm still missing most of the spell and details to say what it's for. I was working on it, waiting for you to get here."

"Oh! That's great. I should copy what you have."

"We can do that. Or you can take a picture. I don't have a scanner."

"That'll work."

"I'm fixing to make dinner. I didn't want to start too early, but I wasn't 100% sold on what I wanted to cook either. I was thinking of soup in bread bowls? Or chicken?"

"Either would be fine, though I love bread."

"Soup and bread bowls, it is. Broccoli cheddar soup okay?"

"Yep."

I got lost looking at what he had colored in on the spell page. It was detailed, and easily something I would buy as art to hang on my wall. Getting past the drawn items, though, I read the list itself. Some of the ingredients I hadn't heard of before.

"This is beautiful. You do amazing work."

"Thanks. It's relaxing, honestly. I'm glad to have been working on it."

"Oh, did any of my students drop by who I recommended?"

"Yep. Hired three of them. They start next week. Thanks."

"That's amazing!"

I snapped a picture, realizing that my hands were clammy, and started to sit down on the chair, but my bulky jacket was in the way.

"Oh, here, let me get your coat and scarf. We can hang them up here."

I took them off and turned to hand them to him. His eyes landed on my shirt and traveled down the rest of me, lingering in certain areas. I'd like to say I was insulted, but really I felt a thrill run through me.

"You look amazing. I love the stars."

"Thanks. It felt nice."

No way I was telling Piper and Tess made me do all this for our "date".

I sat down and placed my hands on my knees. I was trying to decide whether I was just going to bring it up. Winston moved and sat in the only other chair that was at the dining room table. He looked amazing, wearing a dark gray t-shirt, and blue jeans.

"So. We should talk." I finally said.

"You said you had something you wanted to bring up before. What is it?"

"I'm not a witch." I blurted out.

Winston cocked his head to the side. "I know?"

"And you said you wanted to go on a date. And then you kissed me."

"I... also know that?" Winston smiled, but was clearly confused.

"I'm messing all this up. Just..."

I blew out a deep breath and squared my shoulders. "I realize this is probably a far off matter, if ever, but I like to know what I'm getting into. I have a much smaller chance of giving you future witches if we were to marry and have kids. Doesn't that matter to you?"

He slumped back into his chair.

"Ah. That."

"Yeah. That."

I wrung my hands together. He leaned forward, reached out a hand and placed it on mine. It was so warm.

"Listen. I've known this all my life. When your mother is on the council, witch details, growth rates, and other issues are common dinner talk. Hell, my mother was trying to get me into an arranged marriage a month ago. I would prefer to marry for love than for anything else. And whatever and whoever my children are, is in the future. And it'll be okay if they aren't witches. I knew what I was doing when I asked you on a date. Mostly."

"Mostly?" my voice squeaked.

"Well, I had meant to wait until after the whole deadline or favor thing. I just got a bit ahead of myself."

"Oh, yeah. That's why I didn't say yes."

"Is that the only reason?"

"Mostly."

"To be truthful, the only thing I might regret is my mother." Winston shrugged his shoulders and winced.

"Your mother?"

"She's going to be a pain, most likely, and I'll just apologize up front for it. My mother is strongly opinionated and wants what is best for us... but sometimes loses sight of what that should mean."

"Great. I can't wait to meet her." I took his hands in mine.. "You sure? This seems like an enormous thing to decide."

"Willow. I've only known you for like a week. And I think about you constantly. I created food for you. I remember your schedule. I'm entranced. And no woman has ever done that to me before, witch or not. I want to explore this relationship."

I glanced up and saw Winston intently watching me.

"Okay." Feeling awkward, I changed the subject to the first thing I thought of, "So how about dinner?"

Chapter 14

Winston

Willow had looked stunning when she'd walk through my door. I'd been silently repeating in my head that even if we had talked, I couldn't kiss her yet. She wasn't ready to do that again, or at least hadn't said so, and I wanted to respect that. But I also wanted to kiss her until she begged for more.

Instead, I focused on our tasks, and her clear love of food. Why couldn't the way to a woman's heart be through her stomach?

"You've already seen my work. Let me show you a couple of things?"

Looking over the spell sheet with Willow, I showed her the different pieces I had drawn and colored in over what was there. The wording of the spell itself had been traced out, and I'd written the ingredients on a separate piece of paper.

"I'll admit that I had to call my mother about two of these. She's supposed to get back to me on the third. So, the first is Skin of Man, which is actually Fern leaf, and the second is Semen of Hermes, which is –"

"Dill," we said together, Willow looking up at me.

"I recognize that." She replied. "I don't understand why this was all so hard to make out before. And I see you noted Blind Eyes is poppy. So the fourth... Joy of the Mountain?"

"That's the one my mom didn't know offhand. Which is odd."

"Interesting..."

Willow said nothing as she pulled out her own notes and started looking over the spell wording. I watched for a few minutes before finally excusing myself.

I left Willow and went downstairs to the kitchen. She had known about the issues with witches and children... and that had been part of why she had run. It made more sense now. We were so new to each other, and I'd rushed straight in when I hadn't mean to. I'd just lost all control. That said, even though we still needed to talk, I was firm in my belief that I wanted to have a relationship with her. I *wanted* her, in more ways than one.

I needed to make dinner, and she wanted to work on the spell. The kitchen was warm and soothing. The smells of baked bread, coffee and sweets always centered me. I'd prepped both options, so I just pulled out the ingredients I'd set aside in the fridge and pantry, and grabbed the stew pot.

In no time at all, the soup was simmering on the stove, and I pulled the bread bowls from the oven where I'd been keeping them warm. I ladled soup, grabbed spoons, and headed back upstairs with the wooden tray loaded with our meal. I had wine in the fridge upstairs already. I didn't even stop to make sure Lyzzie was doing okay in the café. Even after only a few days, I trusted my two main employees to handle themselves, or get me if they needed.

Willow had propped up her feet on the chair across from her that I'd been sitting in and was texting something on her phone.

"Tell Piper all about it?" I asked, joking, as I sat the food down on the kitchen counter.

Her blush traveled from her chest all the way up to her cheeks. "No?"

"Hmmm," I said, trying not to laugh as I piled all the papers up and moved them out of our way. "I somehow don't believe that." I grabbed the wine glasses and wine, adding them to the tray. I also grabbed two bottles of water. Important to stay hydrated.

I sat the food down on the table, and Willow sat up straight, dropping her feet to the ground.

"That smells like heaven." I could see her actually sniffing the air.

With a smile, I sat down across from her. "You know, I love how much you love my baking and cooking."

She smiled sheepishly. "I've always loved food." She reached up and pulled some pins from her hair, shaking it out. "Sorry, it was starting to give me a headache."

"Don't apologize, your hair is gorgeous down too. And comfort matters. Do you need anything for the headache?" I watched as she ran her fingers through her hair to untangle it and resisted the urge to grab her and kiss her again, or just to even reach out with my own hand and do the same.

"No," she said, and paused. "Actually, you know what? If you have any of the stuff you made Charlotte, I'd take it. I try to fight off my own headaches, but it doesn't always work. I don't want to deal with it tonight."

"Yeah, give me a second! I made a couple of vials to keep on hand."

I went to my cabinets in the kitchen and found the vial I needed. I handed it to Willow.

"Just a swallow of it should work. You can keep the rest, if you want."

"I love magic," she said, after taking a small sip. She corked it back, and slid it into the side of her backpack.

She smiled that beautiful smile at me, and we started eating.

"I feel bad about how many times you have fed me such delicious food, and you keep working on these spells. I've barely done anything for you."

"We've had this discussion. It's fine. What is more important to me is knowing that you didn't run away from my kiss because you were repulsed by me."

I looked intently at Willow, feeling the heat that she called to life within me. Willow almost dropped her spoon, but she persevered and took another bite. Then she tore off a piece from the top of the bread bowl and dunked it in.

"I had a bad experience with someone in college. Two someones actually. The first guy... We'd dated for a year, and I thought he was the one. We got engaged... and from there it quickly went downhill. He'd been cheating on me, and well, that was the tip of the iceberg. I broke it off and went from that to dating a woman who I literally worshiped. She took my heart and shredded it. Honestly, I haven't even dated that much since, or before. We only just met. It was a mix of panic, worry you'd regret it, and the fact that we were working together on a project that is important to me."

"I didn't mean to ask you to date me until after the project. Or to kiss you, really. I just... did."

She smiled and shook her head. "Yeah, cause I'm so irresistible."

I couldn't help it. "You're kidding right? You are hot, Willow, and there is not a second we are together that I do not want to grab you, shove you against a wall and kiss you senseless."

Realizing the words that had just come out of my mouth, I almost hightailed it out of my apartment.

Willow did drop her spoon then, and her mouth formed "Oh," but she didn't say anything.

It took all my strength to not follow through with exactly what I had just described.

Instead, I clenched my fist in my lap and I cleared my throat. "So um, yeah. That."

Willow closed her mouth and then took another bite. This time she managed to say "Oh" aloud.

"Sorry, I..."

"No, it's... it's okay. Nice to know, I suppose."

"Heh." I said, not sure how to respond. There was only so much I could say without losing it. I felt the tension like a knife.

Willow finally spoke, "I'm sorry that I ran from you. And I'm glad that we've talked. It's hard for me to imagine you not caring that you'll possibly squander your chances to carry your magical line with me."

"And yet, so much that I might gain. And it isn't guaranteed that I will not have a witch child. Just lower chances."

"I know. Still. I can see your mother's viewpoint. I would love to have magic myself."

"Is that why you study the history of it? And have a best friend who is a witch?"

"Part of it. But we were friends long before it mattered. We grew up together. Her house was across from mine, and our birthdays are only a month apart."

"Sounds like a fun childhood."

"It was. And I loved magic. Some of my family had it, but not all."

"Some? So you have magic in your genes?"

Willow pondered at that, and shook her head. "If I recall right, they married into the family. And it was a bit of an uproar. My family doesn't approve of magic. They weren't thrilled I was best friends with Piper, either."

"But you study it?"

"I lied to my parents while I was in college about what I was studying. They didn't really ask a lot of questions, and if they knew they'd pull my funding. My dad wasn't the best, and honestly I'd planned to cut ties anyway–I also just wanted access to the savings account they'd filled in for me. So I did. And then I told them the truth."

"And it didn't go well?"

"Not really. I have an uncle I still talk to occasionally, but I haven't spoken with my parents in years."

Putting down my spoon, I reach out and put my hand on Willow's knee. "I'm sorry they were like that."

"I've long come to terms with it. There are things that hurt occasionally. Memories dredged up from the bottom of the barrel that make me weep. But mostly, I do okay with it."

"Still... that sucks."

We were silent for a moment, and I ate some more, thinking about what that kind of family can be like. Those born without magic often resented those who had it. It could be complicated, to say the least. My mother had recounted stories of families coming before the witch council to have magic levels tested, and even people getting DNA tests to check whether or not they belonged.

"Not to change the subject," Willow smiled sheepishly, "but it'll be a couple of hours before we can brew the potion, right? I can happily keep working on this other spell. I think I'm close to figuring out the instruction text on it. I don't want to bore you, though."

"You do whatever you want or need. Don't worry about me. I'm in my house/café after all. I can find a way to busy myself."

For the rest of the meal, we talked about her day, and mine. When we'd finished eating, and I'd cleared the trays, I poured us a little more wine, and smiled.

"You work, and I'll get out of your way. I'll let you know when it's time?"

"That'd be amazing. Thanks, Winston."

Grabbing my tray, I went and put it on the counter. Then I brought all the papers I'd moved before back to the table. As I was setting them down, she stood up a bit and kissed me on the cheek. I put my hand on her cheek, and kissed her forehead. The gentle warmth from her face, and her deep blue eyes beckoned me in. Not wanting to lose myself, I backed away, smiled, and carried the tray downstairs.

After a few hours, the time had finally come for the potion to be brewed. Willow and I stood in the kitchen, with a cauldron and all the ingredients ready. It was more a tea than anything else, but the spell called it an elixir. I looked through the list one more time.

Essence of the Moon, or moon water

5 Rose petals

5 Hibiscus petals

5 Adder's Tongue petals, or Violet petals

1 elf leaf, or lavender, one stalk

2 teaspoons of sugar

A pinch of ground Cloves

Some Black tea leaves

A pinch of ground Cinnamon

"I think this is everything."

"And you really want to brew a potion with me that could show us we are or are not soulmates? It seems like a lot for the start of a relationship. What if we aren't soulmates according to this? Or we can't interpret the results? Will you kiss me again?"

I paused, looking at her. "The most important takeaway I have from that entire ramble is that it sounds like you *want* me to kiss you again."

"I... um... yes." Willow had turned a beautiful shade of pink, flushing up her chest and cheeks.

I leaned down a bit, and took her face in my hands. With a gentleness that took more willpower than I wanted to admit, I kissed her slow and sweet. Then I pulled back, and dropped my hands.

"I promise, that no matter what the spell does, I would happily kiss you everyday. And much more besides. You wanted to know the potion's purpose, did you not? This is really the only way."

Willow looked to the side and into the cauldron. It was enough. She nodded, and I could tell she didn't trust herself to speak.

"Read the instructions to me? We'll work together. I've already opened the shutters, so the light is streaming inside. It's not cloudy, and the moon hits this window, so we don't even have to adjust for that. My aunt's planning of this café was for more than just baking."

Shamelessly, I watched Willow's every movement as she bent over the table to reach for the other copy of the recipe. She turned around and caught me watching her. With a raised eyebrow, she shook her head and started reading.

"First it says to 'brew the moon's essence upon the next full moon by bringing the water to a boil bathed in moonlight.' Okay, so start the fire, and let's boil!"

"I'd prefer not to boil, myself." I joked. She laughed, and I felt warmth fill me.

It wasn't long before the water in the cauldron began to boil on the stove.

Willow continued, "Now it says to 'Bring the cauldron off the fire and add in the ingredients.' I suppose that means all at once."

I grabbed the various items and dumped them unceremoniously into the cauldron that I'd moved to a different burner. I supposed I could be more mystic or careful about it, but it didn't say anything in the instructions, and I was curious to find out what would happen.

"Then," continued Willow, "It says 'after a span of five moments,' which we decided was five minutes, 'pour the tea into the vessels.' Once we've done that we'll 'recite together the verse, sharing the first sip as you lock eyes with one another, weaving the magic together that will show the true nature of your spirits.' Doesn't sound daunting at all."

I laughed softly as I watched the timer on my phone count down. I reached towards the back of the counter and grabbed the two teacups I'd washed and purified earlier today. They were black with the moon phases on them, a set my aunt loved.

"It sounded like a tea, so I thought teacups were appropriate." I smiled at Willow.

"Those are pretty. I think it should work fine. Vessel surely has a lot of room for interpretation."

The timer beeped, and I sat the teacups down. Setting aside the paper, Willow held them in place as I poured from the cauldron.

"Bits and pieces will be in the tea since there was no straining. Be prepared for that."

"It's really pretty," she whispered. "It's pink, and the petals are floating on top."

I sat the cauldron down on the stove with the rest of the items.

"Okay. So next we recite the words," Willow said, moving the sheet between us. "And we need to look at each other as we take the first sip." She paused. "You ready?"

"Yes." I said simply. I had no worries about how this went. I wanted Willow, and magic would not change my mind either way. Together, we chanted:

"With thine heart full and longing,
With desire, and hope twining,
Take a drink my love, my darling,
Take a drink, and see what is meant to be,
Love eternal, and forever,
With your heart full of passion,
Take a drink, together,
under light of full moon,

And see soulmates' desires."

A small glow emanated from the potion and then subsided. I raised my eyebrow.

Willow nodded, looking more entranced.

Her eyes were beautiful, and I had no problem watching her as we drank the tea. It tasted floral and sweet, with a hint of acidity. We looked at each other for a minute, and I felt nothing. And then I saw Willow's hand glowing blue. I raised my hand to find it was the same color.

She reached her hand out at the same time I did, and when we touched, it was like a lightning bolt. That same "Oh" from earlier formed on her mouth.

I couldn't resist it anymore.

I grabbed her and kissed her, sitting the teacup to the side. Hers clattered to the floor.

With a moan, I kissed her like my life depended on it. She was the air and I was suffocating without it. Her lips parted, and I used my tongue to explore, eliciting little moans from her. My hands went to her waist, and I pulled her closer to me. I was lost.

Chapter 15

Willow

Winston kissed me, and as he did so, he grabbed my waist and pulled me to him. I felt fire throughout my whole body, unable to resist him, and not for one second wanting to. I wrapped my arms around him, and ran my hand through his hair, hearing a moan and realizing it was me.

Thank Goddess the café was closed.

Suddenly I felt something hard hit the back of my butt, and realized we'd been backing up slowly into the table. Winston pulled back for a second, eyed me, and then picked me up and plopped me on the table.

"I think you're overdressed," he said, as he unbuttoned my pants and slid them down my legs. I kicked off my shoes, and he let out a small growl that sent shivers down my body.

He looked at me like he'd eat every bite of me. He growled again, kissing me deeply, and I suddenly wondered if he wasn't really a werewolf. My mind was addled. His hands ran up my legs, and the heat of them intensified the fire running through me. His lips and tongue were insistent, and I pulled at his shirt, popping a few of the buttons as I yanked it off him.

He began trailing kisses down my face, to my neck, unbuttoning my shirt slowly as he went and kissing every single inch of me. When he came to the black lace bra, I had a moment of thanks for Piper, and then quickly forgot her as he pushed it aside and took my nipple into his mouth, sucking and flicking it with his tongue.

I was making inhuman moaning sounds and nearly cried when he stopped, taking his mouth off of me. He kept trailing kisses down my body, his hands never once stopping their journey of feeling my skin, my breast. To my legs, down my thighs, and calves. He traced every inch of me, leaving shivers and sparks traveling all over my body.

Then he tugged me closer to the end of the table and looked up at me.

"Time to eat."

I gasped, as he pushed my underwear aside, and licked me, long and slow. That alone nearly sent me over the edge, but as he continued, using his tongue to quickly flick my clit, I wound my fingers through his hair and considered begging him never to stop.

It was like he instantly knew every part of me and used it to his advantage. I couldn't think, could barely breathe, and when he licked me long and slow again, I came completely undone.

As lightning strikes and stars exploded behind my eyes, he began using that mouth in the most unholy ways possible, and I quickly came a second time.

Before he could start again, I pulled at him forcefully and grabbed his pants, unbuttoning them and pushing them down, with his boxers following. His dick was very erect and directly in front of me, so I closed both of my hands around it and began to pump up and down.

The groan that came out of him made me want to do more, but his mouth found mine again, and I was held there. His hands went to my breasts, magically caressing me there to keep the heat building in me, and I used my hands to bring him pleasure.

One of his hands came down on mine, pausing me.

"Do you have protection? I don't have anything."

"Don't worry about it. I'm covered, and free."

"Same."

And then we were kissing again, Winston's hands coming to either side of me on the table. I wrapped my arms around him and felt the tip of him against me. He growled low and deep, and at my moan, he grabbed my ass and picked me up. My legs instantly wrapped around him, my hands in his hair.

With a control I no longer had at that point, he lowered me onto him. The sensation of him inside made me moan his name, and that finally broke his control. He pumped into me, hard and fast, and I screamed my pleasure, biting into his shoulder. We both exploded at the same time, and I felt like I would never come back down from the high.

He leaned for a minute against the table and then picked me back up and carried me up the stairs.

I finally found the energy to whisper, "Where are we going?"

"To bed. I need to do this properly."

"Again? Now?"

"Yes."

I pulled back, and he grunted, holding me level. "You want to?"

"Are you objecting?"

"Well... no, just..."

He smiled wickedly as we reached his door. We went through and he leaned me back against the wall. My legs were still wrapped around his waist. I had no fear he'd drop me.

He kissed me, making my body react and fill with that lightning sensation again. I'd been without it for far too long, and this felt better than any sex I had ever had.

Pulling back from the kiss, he smiled and continued carrying me into the bedroom. He dropped me on the bed, and as I scooted back, I realized he hadn't joined me. He was watching me, his amber eyes sparking with fire, traveling over my body and setting every single piece of me on fire.

I returned the examination, looking at his well-toned arms, down to his legs, and back up. I crooked a figure at him, and he grinned. We both quickly got rid of any clothing we had left on us. My pants and shoes were downstairs, but the rest of it had made it through.

Stripped, Winston leaned back on his knees, and his eyes roamed over my body again. From my toes to my eyes, slowly, and with every bit of satisfaction on his face. Then he almost prowled along the mattress to me, and kissed me before once again trailing those kisses down to other places.

What followed was better than before and had me screaming in pleasure. By the end of it, I was almost a puddle, and felt warm and drowsy all over. We'd switched positions, and I had collapsed on top of him, laying on him like a pillow.

"That... was amazing."

"Hmm, you were pretty awesome yourself."

I could hear the smile in Winston's voice, too tired to move and look at him. He took care of that problem, and shifted me over to fall next to him. Reaching down, he pulled a cover up over the both of us.

"I'd say we could do it again, but I'm not sure I'd survive it at this point," I mumbled into his hair.

He laughed and said, "I'll take up that challenge next time."

But I was already drifting off to sleep. He whispered something, but I was already too deep in sleep to figure out what it was.

I woke up, confused and unsure of what was going on. The sheets felt weird against me. I let my eyes adjust to the dim light and I sat up.

Cold air hit me, and I realized all at once that I was naked and in Winston's bed.

'Oh no. Oh, no. Oh no,' I thought as I remembered the night before.

The talk.

A potion.

The glow.

And then the kiss.

And well, everything from there.

What happened?

I looked over and saw Winston sleeping beside me soundly. My anxiety was rising. Slowly, every so slowly, I slid outside from under the cover, and found my clothing. Then I crept out to the living room.

Inside, I was panicking and trying not to. I liked Winston a lot. It was fine that we slept together... but what if it was because of the potion? I'd seen that glow on our hands. We'd matched.

Did that mean we were soulmates? I knew he'd wanted me, and we'd talked about it. We'd kissed. But had I meant to do it last night? I can't deny I'd had thoughts about it. Piper had surely dressed me for it.

Why was I having so much anxiety over this?

I dressed and realized that my pants and shoes were still in the kitchen.

The kitchen.

Oh Goddess, we had sex on the table. It'd have to be bleached. And purified. Or burned. He made food on it for Goddess' sake.

I sat down on the couch, pants less. I couldn't leave... could I? That seemed wrong. There was probably an alarm I'd set off if I tried to go outside without waking Winston, and I couldn't leave it unset...

Oh, no, Tess! She'd been in the café. It was too cold for her to have gone home on her own. My phone was on the table, and I grabbed it. I had many missed messages from both Tess and Piper.

Cursing my idiocy, I started looking through them. Tess had been trying to get my attention before closing. Piper had been trying to find out what had happened between me and Winston.

Ah, Piper had come and gotten Tess. We hadn't answered them and... there it was. Piper knew exactly what we had been doing.

I leaned my head back and sighed. If it wasn't for the anxiety, I probably was in the most relaxed state I'd been in for months. Flashes of the night kept crossing my mind, and making me want to go wake him up for round three. Why couldn't I just enjoy it?

My phone said it was 3 am.

Even if I knew that witches rarely had any spells that actually swayed matters of the heart, I knew it was possible. There were counts of the witches' high council hiding or destroying certain spells. But was it because of the perception of what could happen or due to it actually changing something?

This was nonsense. I knew better. But what had that glow been? What was the real purpose of the spell? Were we soulmates?

Soulmates. What did that even mean?

My heart was racing, and I felt clammy. I didn't regret tonight at all.

Hmm, okay, maybe doing it on the table had been a bit much, but at the moment, it hadn't even been a question.

I took a deep breath and tried to count.

Was I really ready for this? Did I need to be in another relationship? I mean, it had been years. I deserved to find love again. *Perhaps starting with at least two official dates before I climbed into... onto? A table with him.*

Love? Soulmate... maybe? I had enjoyed these past several days with Winston more than I cared to admit. But we barely knew each other. I couldn't already love him, could I? What would that even be based on? A week's worth of information?

It was too early... late? To be trying to decide these things. I'd wanted a relationship. I wanted him.

I just needed a break. Did I want to go home? No one was there. I could just go back to bed here. Lay beside Winston and see what happened in the morning.

Could I even sleep, though?

Giving up, and trying to relax, I pulled out my laptop. In a few minutes, I'd pulled up my manuscript and was looking over what I had written on the spell so far.

Taking a deep breath, I wrote about the experience of brewing the potion, hearing the spell, and seeing the effect. The decision now would be whether or not I wanted to share the ending. I knew I would not give many details at all of what had occurred. I could feel myself blushing as I thought about it.

By all accounts, and wording, the spell was simply to show whether two people were meant to be together. It didn't really explain what it did when that was the case, however.

This was the problem with oral traditions. It could be that much easier to make something disappear if you could erase all traces. When you stopped talking about something, it was easier to forget when it couldn't be found written down decades later.

Would another witch know? Could I find someone with the knowledge?

Did it matter? I certainly couldn't do it in time for this book. The chapter would say what it said. And should I even publish it like that? I could always be two chapters short. I mean, I had multiple degrees... I could surely bullshit my way out of two chapters.

Lost in thought, I dozed off on the couch.

"Willow?"

I felt a shake and tried to swat Tess away. I didn't want to wake up yet. I was so tired.

"Willow?"

That wasn't Tess.

I sat bolt upright to find myself on a couch, pants less, and nearly throwing my laptop onto the floor.

Winston was standing near me, holding the laptop to keep it from crashing, with a surprised look on his face.

He was also shirtless, and very, very hot.

Oh, and I was pantless.

And we had slept together.

Twice.

"Good morning. Um, may I ask what you are doing out here?"

He didn't say pants less, but I heard it. My brain was short circuiting.

"I... um... Well, I woke up last night. And came out here and dressed, but um, my pants were downstairs... and I was working on my chapter. I fell asleep, I guess."

"Ah. Afraid if you went downstairs you'd bolt?"

"What? No..."

He raised an eyebrow, and his face was just so cute like that.

"Okay, maybe. I might have thought about it."

He smiled. "Well, it's only 5 am. I wake up early for the café, which I'm kind of regretting at the moment. I do, however, want to... um... clean up downstairs before Lyzzie comes in."

"Okay." I said, pausing. "Oh. Oh my Goddess, yes."

I grabbed my laptop from him and closed it, setting it beside me on the couch. Then I stood, and suddenly we were very, very close together.

"Good morning, again." Winston said.

And he kissed me, slow and long. I could feel myself melting into him. I realized that if I didn't say something, we might wind up back in bed.

"Come on," I said, pulling back. "My legs are cold, and I'd really rather not leave the mess."

Winston smiled and grabbed my hand. I followed him downstairs. Was he not having any doubts? He seemed perfectly happy.

The kitchen was a disaster. The potion ingredients were on the counter, the cauldron still sitting on the burner, and the table...

Well, the table looked clean, but I knew otherwise.

I found my pants and shoes and dressed the rest of the way. Winston also grabbed his pants and put them on. With a bottle of disinfectant and some rags, I started cleaning the table while he cleaned up the rest.

Before 5:30, we had the whole place looking brand new. I felt better and relaxed.

And then Lyzzie walked in through the door.

"Oh. Morning." She said.

The smile on her face told me exactly what she was thinking.

Damn.

"Morning, Lyzzie. You're early." Winston sounded fine.

"Oh, yeah. I wanted to make sure everything was stocked. I left a bit early last night since I knew I was coming in this morning and could do it."

"That's fine. I'm heading back upstairs, but I'll be down before we open."

Lyzzie nodded and went through the door into the café. My skin felt hot, and I was sure that my chest and cheeks were the color of a fire engine.

"You okay?"

"Yeah, I'm fine. I just...not a feeling I'm used to it all." I could drown in embarrassment alone.

"Ready to go up?"

"Yeah. Oh, can I grab a muffin?"

"I'll get you one. Want some coffee?"

"Do you need an answer?" I smiled, trying to feel normal.

He chuckled, "Okay, I'll meet you upstairs in a minute, then."

I took the exit and headed upstairs to gather my stuff. My phone was still silent, but I didn't expect to have heard from anyone this early. I shot a quick text to Piper.

"Free today? We should discuss."

And a following one to Tess: "I'm heading home soon. See you there."

Neither replied immediately, but I didn't expect it. It wasn't even 6 am on a Saturday.

Winston walked through the door with a muffin and a coffee.

"Oh, I can smell the glorious coffee. Thank you." I grabbed it and took a deep breath in. "Heaven." And then drank several sips.

Winston walked over to the dining table and took a bite of another muffin.

"I need to head home. One, I really want a shower, and a change of clothes, but two, I'm not sure Tess got home okay last night." I started eating my delicious muffin.

Winston took another bite of his muffin and nodded. "I can work on the other spell some today. I think we can finish it in time."

"Thank you. Please don't stress out about it. I've decided if needed, I can figure out something to fill it in with. I would like to know, though."

"Text you later?"

"Sounds good. I'll see you later."

I grabbed my backpack and nearly ran out of the back of the café. I couldn't believe that I'd handled that calmly enough. The walk home was brisk, and I was glad for my jacket. My home was quiet, and it looked like Tess wasn't there. Opening the door, I walked in and dropped my bag by the door. Then I started the fire, went and changed, and came back to collapse on the couch.

At eight, my phone dinged with messages from Tess and Piper, waking me up from the light doze I was in.

Piper's pulled up first: On my way with snacks and ready to hear every single last detail. Tess is with me, no worries.

I laughed, ready to talk about it all. If anyone could help me figure out my feelings, it would be those two. And maybe Piper could help me understand exactly why I panicked when I woke up this morning.

Piper's place was 10 minutes away, and I knew she'd probably go faster than she should. Stretching, I felt my body ease, and I got some water to drink. Then I made some jam on toast, and gathered a few of my own snacks to contribute to the breakfast. And a nice pot of coffee.

With water and a large cup of coffee, I sat on the couch again and wrapped myself up in a blanket. Sure enough, Piper arrived with Tess in tow, both demanding news.

"Let the story begin! Tell me every single second."

"Who said I wanted to share?"

Tess laughed. "I refuse to let you leave until you tell me if Winston is as great in bed as he looks."

"I believe I was promised snacks."

"Snacks indeed." Piper came in, setting several bags on the table. I was handed a bag of my favorite gummies.

"Bit early in the morning." I joked.

"Do you really think so? I never say no to candy."

I laughed, feeling better already. For the next hour, I walked them through my day. And everything after.

There were appropriate gasps, laughs, and happy sighs. Plus way too many questions. I answered some of them the best I could.

"Did you want to sleep with him last night?"

"I mean, I guess in a way, I planned for it, right? But it was really quickly decided once we kissed. Maybe I shouldn't have... but I don't regret it."

Tess sighed. "Why would you? It sounded like heaven."

"Not arguing that point, really."

"The potion...You said you glowed? And then your hands, both the same color."

"Yes. And it was... electric."

Piper sat back in thought, eating another piece of candy. "Love spells have been banned by the witches' council for my entire life. They always cause trouble, no matter what your intentions are—good or bad. Really, they may not want you to publish anything about this spell."

"I've never cleared anything with them before."

"No, but you've never published anything dangerous, or that went against what they wanted people to know."

"And how would I even know if I did?"

"Well, witches are everywhere. They keep an eye out for this stuff. And you said your man's mother is a council member."

"How did I not make that connection?"

"I mean, Sullivan in general is a pretty common name. And his aunt wanted nothing to do with it."

I rubbed my hands along the blanket covering my lap. This was getting more and more complicated.

Then I remembered his smile and last night, and realized I didn't care.

And realized that I'd just thought "fall in love" instead of like?

"Can't anything ever be easy?"

"Not the good stuff, darling. You have to work at that."

Tess flew off and grabbed a piece of chocolate. "I wonder if they watch you. Because you aren't a witch and do all this witchy stuff."

I turned toward Piper, taking a drink of coffee. "What do you think?"

"They might. It seems logical. I mean, witches are a part of society, but that doesn't mean we haven't done damage control before. Or tried to figure out how to make certain things go away quicker. Everyone has scandals, right?"

Nodding, I took a bite of a chip. "Everyone does."

Tess didn't say anything, just flew back to the couch. The living room was really warm, and she didn't have any problems flying around.

Groaning, I leaned my head back against the cushion.

"I don't want to write more history into this book. I mean, it wasn't to cause love. Or even to create passion. What do witches think about soulmates?"

"Just the same thing as everyone else. There is someone for everyone—one person who is meant for you, the other half of your soul. I can easily see someone trying to create a potion to figure out whether someone is."

"So why would they have hid that? Perhaps it was too much for them? Think about it. If you could find out whether the person you are interested in is the person you wanted to be with, could you resist it? Then what if word spreads, and everyone wants to know? I mean... this spell could certainly cause chaos."

Piper got up and walked around the couch, into the kitchen. I could hear her pouring her some coffee as she talked.

"Really, any spell could. I mean, we have potions and spells for clear skin, fine weather, and so many other things."

"Thanks. I think. So, what did you two do last night?"

The conversation switched gears for a while as Piper and Tess filled me in on their night. It had been their own version of a girl's night without me there. I was glad that Tess had someone else who could help her.

"I'm glad it's the weekend. So glad that I don't have to go to the office for two days." Piper was eating her own bag of gummies.

"Hard cases lately?"

"No, not really. There's a coworker who has been driving me a bit up the wall. I think she'll be switching jobs soon."

"Ack. Those are the worst. In academics, we just are stuck with them forever. Not much job hopping for professors, once they are on tenure track."

"So, what's your plan today?"

"Well... Winston is going to text me at some point. And other than that, I don't have plans till this evening. Wanna have a girls' day?"

"Absolutely. Let's go shopping. Go put on some real clothes."

Tess cheered, and I gave in. I went to my closet and picked my outfit. Black jeans, and a long cozy sweater. Then my favorite, comfiest pair of black boots. It was nice to wear "Slack off" clothes, as I called them. Business, and even business casual, could take all the fun out of fashion if you weren't careful.

The rest of the day passed quickly, with shopping, pampering, and eating lunch. I felt guilty not being at the café and spending my money somewhere else.

Finally, at around 5 pm, I got a text from Winston.

"Made progress. Come over anytime."

I showed it to Piper and Tess.

"You going? Oh, pack clothes."

"I... don't you think that's forward?"

"Eh, why not? At least a robe, maybe? Oh, come on. If you already did it once, no reason to not do it again!"

She had a point there.

Chapter 16
Winston

The day had passed quicker than I'd expected. I'd worked in the café, but I'd also spent time on the spell. That is, when I wasn't freaking out a bit.

Hard not to think about that. I'd nearly lost track of recipes and orders multiple times during the day, from getting lost in flashbacks of last night. Thank Goddess jeans helped hide some of my reactions.

I'd never been this enamored... or in love. But what had been the effect of that spell? Were we soulmates? Our colors had matched, and that jolt of electricity had made my skin feel on fire... Had it been responsible for the urge I'd had to take her, then and there? Had I ever felt passion like that before?

Had she really wanted it or had the spell also been responsible for how fast we had fallen? She'd seemed out of sorts this morning. Was she regretting our decision? Did she feel trapped? Had she questioned the spell?

I was a witch, and I was scared that I'd caused something to happen. That I'd changed her mind or rushed her into things through magic. Love... love was a tricky thing. Witches had messed with it in the past because it was hard to resist.

Most of the time, nothing happened. But occasionally spells or potions, or both combined, could do something that everyone would desire–or at least the person asking for it. Would people want to get their hands on this for the information? Would it cause a rush towards witches who could perform it? And how could we find out what the meaning had been? Did it really prove that we were soulmates?

I made headway on the other spell, so I texted Willow and heard back that she was on her way. This time she wasn't avoiding me at least. Thinking food would be a good idea, I started cooking us some cheeseburgers.

Willow arrived on my doorstep and didn't bring up this morning past a simple kiss for hello. All I wanted was to take her upstairs, but she seemed to have other ideas.

"It is still mostly the full moon, right?"

Willow's voice broke through the running thoughts in my head, and I realized I hadn't been paying attention. I didn't care one whit about figuring out a spell more than I did wanting to make delicious noises come from her again.

"I'm sorry, what?"

"It's just... Well, I had an idea. It's still mostly the full moon, right?"

"Well. It's not the full, full moon, but close. Why?"

"Would the spell still work? Isn't it common that spells for the full moon can work the whole week? Could you and Piper try it together?"

"Wait, what?"

"Listen, we don't know what the effect was. Not fully. If you and Piper do it, and your color is the same, but hers is different, then we are closer to an answer. And if nothing else seems to happen..."

"As ideas go, it's not a terrible one, honestly. And you could still be present. I don't think it affects you unless you drink it."

"Seems like a good idea. Why couldn't it just like show you a picture of your soulmate or something? Give you a name? Seems a much better idea overall. Clear instructions would have also been great."

"Spells live in the world of vague intentions and near misses. It's easier for the magic to work that way than in precision for something like this. Plus, if you don't write everything down, it can't be stolen."

I shrugged and sat down at the kitchen table where I'd already sat out the food. Willow noticed, and joined me, taking a bite out of the quick sandwich I'd grabbed with some chips.

"Let me text Piper and see what she says. I don't know why I didn't think of this before. I should have had her here last..."

Willow trailed off, not finishing that sentence. Thinking about what happened last night, and how it could have changed with Piper's presence, made me curious whether Willow wished Piper had been here to knock some sense into us, or was very glad she hadn't been.

I still couldn't look at my kitchen table without wanting to grab Willow and throw her on top of it again.

Not healthy. Or perhaps just what I needed.

"She's game. She says I can't..." Willow trailed off. Willow turned beet red and shook her head, hiding her phone. "Um, she just says I have to stay present."

"Good idea. Okay, I still have all the ingredients. We'll get ready for it in a few hours, then."

"Thanks again for everything. You've been such an enormous help. And always willing and ready to do whatever I ask."

"Of course. I'm happy to help. And I think I've made out just fair in this deal."

Willow's blush was turning me on. I had problems. Time to change the subject. "Okay, let's talk about the other spell, then. I think I figured out what it is for."

"Oh, really? What?"

"Invisibility."

"Now that sounds interesting. I don't think I've seen anything about that before."

"Might explain why both spells were hidden in another grimoire, and hard to read. They weren't really allowed. Love spells of any variety have always been frowned upon. Invisibility can lead to too many questions and bad intentions. I mean, think of the robbers and assassins."

"I'm really beginning to think I won't be able to publish either of these spells, and I need to. I mean, I dislike the idea of hiding something away from everyone. I have so many issues with hiding abilities and trying to keep people from knowing what you can do."

"Can you blame them? If people burn you at the stake because they think you are capable of something, you hide pieces of yourself to stay safe."

"If people could just be nice and quit trying to persecute everyone, then it would be much nicer."

"Wouldn't it?"

We both paused and looked at each other. I was happy to sit here and just watch her. Having these conversations about a part of my life she was interested in, and willing to learn more about... it opened up more doors than I thought possible.

"Okay. So what do we want to do now? Want to compare notes on the new spell? I'll run upstairs and grab it."

"Sounds great."

Deciding to avoid taking her near my room was a good goal, so I ran up and collected the notes. I spread them on the kitchen table, pointing to the words.

"Here's the incantation:

'I need to walk in between,
I must travel unseen,
With skin of man, and red wine,
Bring to me the protection of thine,
Joy of mountain, and blind eyes,
Hide me in disguise,
Semen of Hermes, and red wine,
With a ring of this twine,
Let me walk in between,
Let me travel unseen.'

The problem is the direction, and that we are still missing that one ingredient..."

Together, we delved into the work.

Eventually, we leaned back in our chairs. We'd figured out the potion directions - minus the one ingredient.

I twirled my own pencil in my hand, pondering. "I hate to say this, but you might be better off if I call my mother now."

"Better off?" Willow looked tense, and I was worried this would scare her off.

"She's on the council. I should have told you, but what with the last name... most people know who I'm related to without me bringing it up. Of course, I'm usually near the seat of the council. I didn't really think about it. But she might know more about what we are dealing with here. "

"Do you want me to ask her permission?" Her forehead creased, and I could see the doubt starting to take hold.

I shook my head. "It isn't just that. I don't mind what you do - publish it or not. Heck, there might be copies in the archives with more information. Maybe I could get you access. That, and I'd hate for you to deal with consequences you don't have to."

Willow's eyes lit up at that. "Consequences? And I never dreamed of seeing that. They only let high ranking witches on the council, and in the rooms."

"Yeah, well. I have an in. Not that I'm making any promises. It'd be a hard sell. But we need to know these things—and if they don't have copies of these, they will want them. And to know how you got them. It's leverage."

Willow stopped typing something on her computer and looked up. "I found the book at an estate sale a few years ago. Started looking through it. I've found several things that way. I bought it for like two dollars. Does that matter?"

"It might. I never much got mixed up in council business. I know my mom is a stickler for the rules, though."

Putting her head into her hands, I could hear her sigh. Her hair was falling out of her ponytail, and she seemed extra annoyed. I reached out and laid my hand on her knee.

"Hey, listen. I want to help. I'm here, okay? I won't call her unless you want me to."

My body felt tight. I was so tense. I couldn't think, because all I really wanted was to take Willow up to my room and make love to her again. Make all her tension go away. But we had things to do... and I still wasn't sure if last night was going to be repeated.

What had happened with that potion?

Were we soulmates? Were we incompatible? Did it make us do what we did last night?

I had no answers, and it was frustrating to the core. I needed to speak with Willow about it. Soon, though, we'd be doing the same thing with Piper. I was terrified and curious.

When Piper and Tess arrived, I had already once again sat out all the needed ingredients and had the cauldron on the stove. Willow had avoided that end of the kitchen table, and she blushed every time she looked at it.

She was so incredibly adorable.

Tess flitted over to the oven, and sat on the back of it, soaking in the warmth.

Piper walked over and hugged Willow, whispering something into her ear. Willow smacked her, and Piper just laughed.

"So, if I want to jump his bones after this, you'll stop me, correct?" Piper asked her out loud.

"*Yes*." Willow answered back, shooting me an apologetic look. "Sorry, I might have told her a few things."

"Only a few? I'll have to up my game."

Piper nearly died laughing at the expression on Willow's face, who'd gone beet red, and was stuttering. Tess laughed so hard, she fell from the back of the oven and had to fly herself back up. I smiled sheepishly at Willow in apology.

When she'd finally recovered, Piper said, "Okay. First, I like you, and you officially have my approval. Second, let's see if last night was a fluke. Show me the spell and potion."

Willow handed it to me, and if looks could kill, we might not have been able to try the spell again.

After a few minutes of careful studying, she said, "It's moonrise. So let's brew, shall we?"

About seven minutes later, we were ready. I pulled down two cleansed cups, and we each stood on either side of the oven.

"Oh, this is great. It's like a standoff." Tess laughed from the oven.

Willow tried not to chuckle and lost the battle. "You two do look like you are about to joust each other. Relax."

"Impossible," we said at the same time.

It brought a smile to my face. Piper looked to be fighting a grin.

"Okay. I'll fill our cups, and we can both recite the spell. Then we sip. You ready?" Piper watched me and nodded. I looked at Willow.

"Oh, I'm actually recording on my phone. So, let's go. If you make any move to kiss her, I'm punching you."

"Who me?" I asked in alarm. "And I don't want to!"

"Thanks, appreciate that," Piper said dryly. "Come on, we don't want to ruin it."

So I poured the tea, and then together Piper and I recited the spell and drank the liquid. I was thankful that it did not actually taste bad. Some of these potions could make you barf at first taste, and if it had, I wasn't sure I'd willingly repeat it.

It took no time at all for my hands to glow that same blue color—but Piper's had turned a bright red.

"Well, that's something," Willow murmured from behind her camera.

Piper waved her hand in front of me. I watched her do it, still thinking. She broke the silence.

"Sorry bucko. I don't want to jump your bones. So this somewhat helps your theory—I wonder if there are more colors than 2, or just yes and no?"

"Can we touch?" I asked. Willow narrowed her eyes at me, as did Piper and Tess. "No! I don't want to do anything, I just want to see if that spark happens."

Piper shrugged, "I'm game."

And before I could do anything, she poked my hand, then grasped it. And nothing happened.

"In summary," Piper stated, "our colors were different. I feel no... urge to jump his bones. Mostly. Mission accomplished, you two have fun."

"*Mostly?*" I asked.

She smiled wickedly at me, "You are hot. But Willow had dibs."

I stammered, but was cut off by Willow shaking her head, and I saw her end the recording.

"Cool. So, who is next as a guinea pig?" Piper asked, turning to Willow.

Willow shook her head again. "I can't just start testing this on random people. I'd have to do it as a proper study, which would take time to even get approval for, which I don't have right now. Of course, that doesn't mean I won't want to later."

I raised an eyebrow. "Would that many people be willing?"

"People will do anything for $20. Also, I think this might attract some interesting folks."

"It's more information than I had before. Thanks Piper."

"No thanks to me?" Tess asked, mock shock in her voice.

Willow shook her head and bowed at her. "Thank you, lovely one."

Tess scoffed.

"That's all, folks." Piper said, cutting off the argument I was sure was fixing to happen. "I'm heading home. Come on Tess, I'll take you back to Willow's." Piper turned and looked at Willow. "And you text me details later to catch up."

Willow nodded and waved them off. Together, they left out the door. Willow then turned and held up her cell phone. "I could see the colors on each of your hands on film, which is interesting. Do you want to watch it with me and look at what you can see?"

I nodded and turned off the stove. "I need to clean this up some and then we can head upstairs to do that. Then maybe I can give you some more... details."

Making Willow blush might be one of my new favorite activities. She shyly said, "Maybe." It wasn't a no. I'd take the hope.

She slid the phone into her back pocket, and then helped me clean up the kitchen. Together we made short order of the work, and headed upstairs, where my mind was not at all on the video.

Once there, we watched the video together. Sure enough, there were the glows—two very different colors. And no attraction, whatsoever.

"I remember that blue. It's the same as before, right?"

"Yes, I think so. Which begs the question of is it only blue and red glows, or does each match have their own variation of a color?"

I nodded, and added "Well, that proves that it didn't make us fall into each other as we did. Piper and I had no urges."

"True."

I looked at Willow, and noticed the curve of her lips, and how pretty she looked when she concentrated.

She was so intelligent.

If the spell hadn't caused my mind to become obsessed with her... then how had I already fallen so deeply?

"Dibs, by the way?"

"Please, please, don't ask? I might tell you one day."

I laughed, and shook my head. "That leaves one unanswered question I hate to bring up but feel I must. I can call my mother to confirm now. She should be awake."

Willow worried her lips between her teeth and shook her head. "Let me work on it tonight. If I can't figure it out, we can call tomorrow."

"Okay."

So she was going home then.

"Do you want to look together?" I asked, hopeful. Trying not to reach out and grab her, and kiss her senseless.

"No. I think I'm going to head home. I'm tired, and I'd like to work on these chapters some more. I don't have too much time left for it. But thanks for the offer. I'll text you tomorrow?"

"Yeah. Yeah, that's fine." Then I remembered. "Actually, we've never exchanged numbers. We should probably do that."

"Wait, what?" She scrolled through her contacts. "Huh. Okay. Trade."

She handed me her phone, and I gave her mine. We entered our numbers, and then I walked her to the door, and when she turned and looked up at me, I bent down and gently, slowly kissed her. I didn't want to spook her off.

Willow leaned into me, kissing me back gently. It was a long, slow, kiss that made me burn in all the right places. When she pulled back, leaning against the door, she smiled up at me.

"We should probably stop there."

Goddess help me, her voice sounded husky.

"Want me to walk you home?" My own voice sounded like a growl.

There was a flash of something in Willow's eyes, but then she shook her head.

"No, not tonight. Probably not... the best idea. I'll let you know I get home safe."

"Okay. Good night, Willow."

"Night, Winston."

And just like that, she was out the door and down the sidewalk.

Dragging my heart behind her.

Chapter 17

Willow

I settled in at home, wearing comfy pjs and with a glass of wine, to go through my manuscript and just chill. The past week had been nothing but eventful, and my brain was on overdrive, and refusing to function all at once.

Tess had gone with Piper again, so I was alone in the house. It was quiet, with just the gentle piano music I had playing, and the crackling of the fire. I should grade or check my emails or do any number of things. Instead, I was daydreaming about Winston's smile.

And, well, other things.

Shaking my head, I ran my hands through my hair for the 80th time. Maybe another glass of wine and a soak in a hot tub was what I needed. With that in mind, I grabbed my laptop and the wine. My bathroom was chilly, so I kicked up the heat and started running hot water into the tub.

With some Epsom salts, and a special bomb Piper had made me, I soon had the relaxing scent of lavender and mint in the air. Bubbles covered the surface of the water, and I eagerly sank down into the bath.

"Ouch, ouch, ouch."

My skin was on fire... but then my body settled out to the temperature, and I felt warm and cozy all over. A hot bath was always the right call, I thought.

I turned on an episode of *Friends* and closed my eyes. Listening to the banter helped calm me, and I relaxed into the bath. My body felt free, and I stayed there, replenishing and heating up the water twice.

Finally, when my skin had wrinkled as much as my body could handle, I drained the water and got out. Unwilling to lose the calm I had gained, I pulled on my pajamas and laid down in bed. Pulling the covers up over me, I went to sleep thinking of a smile and dreamed of a kiss.

The next morning was Sunday, and luckily I didn't have an alarm set. I slept until well in the morning, when my phone went off, and the front door was opening. I sat up, rubbing my eyes.

That had been a good night of sleep.

"Morning!" Tess' voice called from the living room. I threw off the covers and put on my robe. Walking into the living room, I found Tess and Piper.

Piper raised an eyebrow, and looked me up and down.

"I'm taking it, that with that outfit, there isn't a hot guy asleep in your bed or hiding behind curtains?"

"No. I came home last night. Too much on my mind."

"Yeah, yeah, yeah. You need more fun in your life," Tess said, flitting back to the bedroom. I shook my head.

"I need to focus on my book. This is my career, after all."

Piper laughed. "You have been focused on your career for years. Maybe that career is finally trying to find you a love life."

"In the words of Tess, 'yeah, yeah, yeah'. You staying?"

"No, I've got to clean my house, and I desperately need to do laundry. Plus, there aren't any fun new stories to hear here."

"Ah, I'll keep that in mind next time."

"Uh, huh. Toodles, Love. Maybe you'll have better luck tonight."

I shook my head as Piper left. I could have gotten lucky last night based on how Winston was looking at me. But my brain still couldn't completely reconcile the fact that we both seemed head over heels for each other in no time at all. Was this connection truly because we were soulmates?

Or had we done something else to ourselves with magic we didn't understand?

With a whole day ahead of me, I looked towards my kitchen. Piper wasn't the only one who needed to clean. I whistled, and Tess flew back in.

"I don't know what the state of your laundry is, but we need to clean up."

"Dire. So yes, as much as it sucks, I agree."

The next few hours were spent cleaning up the house.

"When did I grocery shop last?" I asked, staring into my fridge, which contained two bottles of wine, a few condiments, and almost nothing else.

"Have you this century?" Tess asked, looking in as well. I thought about closing her in it. The freezer wasn't much better.

"I didn't want to put on clothes today."

"Are you streaking? I thought you had on clothes."

"You know what I mean. But I also want food. So, guess it's time to hit the store."

We shopped, brought the food home, and got it all put up. I made a late lunch, and we decided to continue binge watching *Friends*, as Tess had also watched it multiple times.

Finally, I started grading and handling some of my things for work. It was easy enough with *Friends* in the background, since I knew what was happening on screen anyway. As I caught up on grading, I also pondered what I wanted to do with the book.

I needed to text Winston. Perhaps we should call his mother. Then again, I wondered what I would do if she demanded I not print these spells. Winston wasn't lying about the fact that the council had hidden them numerous times. There had often been reasons for what they did... but did I agree with all of it? Was it okay to hide part of who you are?

If witches had hid the love spells because of issues, what else might they be able to do? Was the other spell really to turn invisible? Could they be hiding even more intense spells in their vault? Did people not just create new ones to do what they needed?

Magic was complex, and it was near impossible to know exactly what enabled any of it to work. Some people could create new spells, and some lacked the ability.

My brain raced in circles. It didn't always make sense. I finally texted Winston and said, "Tomorrow? I think we should speak with your mother. I can come in the afternoon after class."

It only took a few minutes before I heard from him.

"Sure. Works for me."

With that settled, I tried to ignore my anxiety over the decision. There were also a few other witches at the college I could ask... though whether I wanted to do that, I still wasn't sure.

Ah, the complexities of publishing in academia.

The next morning, the café was bustling when I made it there, and once again, Winston instantly made my coffee when he saw me.

This time though, he walked around the counter with it, and a to-go bag with something inside.

"Don't I need to pay?"

"Not here. Now shoo."

I seriously thought about kissing him, but there was quite the audience. I didn't want to hear any comments, so I waved towards Lyzzie and hightailed it out of there. Then I also remembered that he had hired a couple of my current students...

That could get awkward. Both a blessing and curse that he lived over his coffee shop. Coffee all the time, but also... people.

Work went by in a flash, and before I knew it, it was time to head to the café. My feet were killing me, even though these boots were something I wore often enough. Another long, hot bath sounded wonderful. Or a foot massage.

The cool air on my skin felt wonderful after the heat inside. Fun thing about academic buildings—they seemed to either always be way too cold, or 100 degrees. So I always carried a cardigan or light jacket, and even kept a blanket in my office.

I pulled my jacket closer to me and let the wind whip through my hair. My braid had come out a long time ago. The colors were fading, and I needed to re-dye it soon. Piper and I had tried creating a permanent, never-fading dye. It hadn't worked—but we had been able to drastically lengthen the time between dyes.

My mind wandered as my feet followed the normal path. Students waved and said hi or hurried past late to their classes. I missed the almost carefree days of being a college student, or as much as I could be.

I'd been working part time, but thanks to several scholarships, had only needed money for food and extras. It was a lucky thing. Even luckier that Piper roomed with me. She'd been instrumental in helping me recover from my two broken hearts during college.

The two times I'd given my heart away, it'd been abused and destroyed. So why now did I seem so willing to throw it into the hands of someone I barely knew? Why now, when it was tied up in my work, my career, and the things that I valued above all else?

My career, my goals, had been there for me. Nothing was going to keep me away from my dreams, and with dedication I'd been so good at what I do they hadn't been able to deny me the spot. I'd brought in grants, research, and publications, even before I'd been a full professor.

My name was known.

And so was Winston's mom's. I wondered why I hadn't really made the connection. His aunt had never talked much about her personal life.

Classical music drifted on the air, and I realized with a start that I'd made it to the café. I leaned against the fence going up to it and waited. Not really sure what for—but more just to give myself a pause. A moment to drink in what the café looked like and the feelings I felt for it.

Was I falling for the new owner because I'd always been in love with the café? I scoffed at the notion. Not that I wasn't in love with the café—between its location, excellent beverages and food, and dreamy exterior, I'd always loved it. But I didn't think I was silly enough to fall for a guy just because he could make me the perfect muffin.

That thought made my stomach growl. It was time to face the music. I'd be meeting Winston's mother via the phone for the first time, without her even really knowing who I was. What if she recognized my name? What if she got angry I was with her son?

Was I with her son? Would she even know I was there?

I shook my head side to side, trying to make the questions just stop swimming around and chasing each other. Nothing for it, but to go in. And so I did.

The café was slow. Most students were in class, or getting ready to go out. It was that sweet spot in which you could be more alone in your thoughts and have a calmer sip of coffee.

I met Winston at the counter, and he handed over a sandwich and a coffee.

"Maybe I wanted chocolate." I said around a mouthful.

"I mean, I can put chocolate on it, but I don't think it would be very appetizing."

"Whatever. That's your taste."

Winston raised an eyebrow and went to grab his chocolate syrup.

"No, no, just kidding. I'm good with this..." I looked at the sandwich, "Turkey and cheese. Thanks."

I took my food and coffee and plopped at a table by the outside windows. Winston followed.

"What's up? You can come back to the kitchen."

I smiled, but pointed outside. "I love the gardens. I wanted to look at it again before it was buried in snow."

"Good point. Snow is one thing I'm worried about. Didn't really deal with it much in California."

"Don't worry. We can teach you all the ways of us folks who live in too much of it."

He laughed, and I smiled up at him. I took another bite of the sandwich and nodded my approval.

"It's good. Is that special sauce?"

"My recipe. Shhhhh."

With a laugh, I leaned back and finished the sandwich. He waved and headed back to the counter as another customer came in. Whoever was working must be on break.

I wondered if he'd been able to make any headway on the spell. I hadn't, and I'd tried since yesterday. Calling his mother was the only other thing I could think of.

An hour passed by, with me grading and watching the outside world, and Winston helping with the afternoon rush that finally showed. Eventually, I packed up and went to the kitchen. It smelled heavenly, a mix of coffee and bread, and I never wanted to leave it.

There wasn't anything currently baking, but the oven was putting off tons of warmth, so I sat as close as I could to it. The heat made me nearly want to doze, and I think I nodded off when I heard footsteps.

Winston was standing by the door, watching me. The look on his face made me want to jump him, but then he smiled ever so slightly, and walked closer.

"Hey, you awake?"

"Yeah, sorry. Heat was making me drowsy, and it's been a long day."

"Say no more, I understand. So good news, bad news. I haven't found out much, but I'm sure my mother can help. It's a good time to call her now."

Breathe in, breathe out. Repeat.

"Willow?"

"Yeah. Sorry. Okay. Yeah. We can call your mom. Does she have to know I'm here?"

"Not really. Is there a reason she shouldn't?"

"Not all witches like me. Also, I'm not sure I'm at the 'meet the parents' stage yet."

Winston choked back a laugh, and said, "Yeah, I'm not sure you'll ever want to actually meet my mom. I'm going to say again that she can be intense. Especially where I'm concerned. My brother married a witch and has two kids already. I'm not holding up my end of the bargain. So if she says anything, please be prepared."

"Noted. And mums the word here."

Winston nodded and pulled out his cell. He thumbed through and then hit something on the screen. A few minutes later, a ringing sound came out of the phone. Each one was like a poke to the heart.

Finally, a woman's voice answered.

"Winston? Is that you?"

"Yes, Mom. I was calling for some advice."

"Advice? You could just call to talk to me, you know."

"Sorry, Mom. Things have just been busy with the café and all. You know how running a business can be."

"Not for those without magic. So, what do you need advice for?"

"I told you I was working on a couple of spells for someone. I need help deciphering one or seeing if we have a copy in the vault."

"Now, who said I was willing to go into the vault?"

"Mother. Come on."

"What does the spell do?"

"I'm not sure. We think maybe invisibility."

"And she wants to publish that? What was the other one?"

Winston winced. "Well, that was more complicated..."

"Winston Charles Sullivan, you tell me right this instant."

"It was a love spell, of a sort."

I hear a gasp over the phone. "Explain of a sort."

My mother's voice was cold steel.

"It identifies whether the person doing it with you is your soulmate."

"How?"

"It appears that your hands glow the same color. Or at least that is what we think."

"I see. She cannot publish that."

I almost make a protest, but remember she does not know I'm listening. It takes all my might and willpower and nearly breaking skin with my nails as I clenched my fists, but I keep quiet.

"Why Mom? It doesn't make anyone love anyone."

"Are you sure about that? Does it outline anything? We'd need to examine it further. And a spell for invisibility? If that works, it can create havoc."

"Mom, we already have so many spells that could wreak havoc. Why do these two matter?"

"Send me pictures. I shall examine them and call you back in an hour."

"Promise?"

"I promise to look, I don't promise to share any details. Now quit whining and do what you are told."

"Okay, okay, going. Bye Mom."

Winston hung up the phone and sat it down on the table. His shoulders hunched in, and he looked defeated.

"Honestly, that wasn't as bad as I feared."

He looked up at me, hope in his eyes. "Do you want to send her the pictures?"

I looked away, and then down at my hands. Did I? I'd avoided getting help from the witches in the department because they would demand credit, and I wasn't really fond of most of them. But his mother? A council member? I could offer a thank you to them, and it probably wouldn't matter.

Or she could demand everything, and I'd have a fight on my hands.

That said, I had little choice at this point. I'd never been so confounded before. And Winston's magic wasn't even helping him.

"Yes. I think so."

Winston held a hand out in front of him, towards the stairs to his apartment. "My copies are upstairs. I can snap some pictures."

"You go ahead. I am really enjoying the warmth."

Winston smiled finally and nodded. He raced up the stairs, his long legs skipping steps as he went. I shuffled closer to the oven and tried to put my brain to rights. I was torn between wanting to rip the papers to shred, finding out every detail possible, and throwing myself at Winston in a fit of passion.

What even was my brain lately?

Winston came back down, and I looked up. "Sent," he said. "Want to help me with the dinner rush?"

There wasn't anything more I could do with the book for now, so I nodded, and took the apron he handed me. Maybe the quiet calm in the bakery would help settle my racing heart. Or coffee.

Chapter 18

Winston

My mother always rattled me. I never knew how she was going to act. Sometimes she doted on me, and other times she acted like I was an idiot who needed all the guidance possible. Add in a girlfriend, and the mix just got odder.

I dreaded introducing Willow to my mother. Even letting her hear my mother talk to me was humiliating since she always made me sound stupid. We weren't in a good spot right now, and things had been tense.

Trying to ignore that, I settled into the comfort I had found in running the café. Willow helped in the kitchen, and we managed to get everything I needed for the evening and morning ready to go. With the time, I even managed to prep several things for the week. Maybe I could take the chance and sleep in.

"When do the new kids start?" Willow asked, looking at Charlotte working the register.

"Today, actually. One is coming in for a couple of hours to watch closing and going to work all of tomorrow evening. Another is starting in the morning with Lyzzie.

I haven't nailed down the third's schedule yet. Charlotte and Lyzzie are both excellent at their jobs, and I've given them a raise for training the new folks."

"That's amazing! I'm happy to hear it. I'm glad you've gotten help. Hopefully, some of them can bake too."

"Two of them have at least some experience. Lyzzie also can do more than I knew, so we're going to start working on rotation when she's in here with me in the kitchen, and two others are out there. My aunt also let me in on that secret. You pre-make it and freeze it. Then they just throw it in the oven and follow directions. Or prep for the week where it's much easier to toss things together."

"Genius." Willow said, laughing.

I nodded. "I need to do it for me, too. I know there will be days I won't be able to manage or want to go some-where. Days when things are busier than I expected and we'll need more food. It's a good idea."

Willow was about to ask something else, and I realized I was staring at her lips. I was just thinking of all the things I could do, when my phone rang. Damn it.

Feeling awkward, I looked at the screen and saw it was my mother. I held it up for Willow to see and put my finger to my lips.

A blush crept up her cheeks. That had me wishing I really did not have to talk to my mother right then. The thoughts alone in my head were not ones I'd ever want my mother to know about. It felt extra awkward answering the phone, as I tried to shove those memories out of my mind.

I answered the call, putting it on speakerphone.

"Hello? Mom?"

"Winston? I've looked over what you have sent me. That spell cannot be published. You can tell the witch it'll be a council command, but if she goes against it, we'll revoke it."

I looked at Willow, and her eyes were huge. I waved my hand at her to get her attention. She just shook her head no.

"Why can't she publish it? It doesn't have anything to do with conjuring love."

"Do we know that for sure? It needs to be done, several times, to see the results of it. Even then, I'm not sure it's a service or spell we'd want to advertise. It could cause some major backlash in the world of dating apps."

"Dating Apps?"

"Love is a business. And many people are happy thinking they are with their soulmate. If they could know for certain? If you've been married for ten years and find out your spouse isn't? Disasters waiting to happen."

Willow looked thoughtful at that, but still angry. She waved her hand in the air. I shook my head.

"Ignoring the arguments I have about that, what about the second one?"

"We are examining it now. It is going to take longer than I expected."

"Is it for invisibility?"

"We aren't sure yet. We're checking the archives. I'll get back in touch when we know something. You convince that witch of yours that if she knows what is good for her that she doesn't need to publish either of them."

"I don't know that I can. What happens if I don't?"

"If it's a council sanction to hide these spells, we'll revoke her ability to practice in a public manner. Which would make teaching magic extremely difficult for her, and the college probably wouldn't want to continue being associated with her."

"That seems a bit extreme."

"Hundreds of years have been spent carefully avoiding disasters. Even with the best efforts of the council, things happen. We can't afford to risk it."

"I understand that, but neither of these—,"

She cut me off. "Convince her, if you know what's good for both of you."

And she hung up. Great. I stared at the phone in my hand, afraid to meet Willow's eyes. I finally looked up.

Willow's eyes were huge. Her hands were twisting together, and she looked as if she might scream at any second. Or blow a top like they did in cartoons.

"Willow, I'm sorry. My mother is very used to getting her way."

"I can tell. But what if I try to publish it?"

"She'll probably find a way to stop you. I have no idea what all the council is capable of. I should have paid more attention, but when your mom is in charge, you kind of try to avoid it."

Willow tapped the table in front of her, deep concentration showing on her face. I would wait and see what she decided. I wasn't sure how to persuade her either way on whether to publish or not.

"Wait... 'that witch of yours'—what did she mean by that?"

My heart skipped a bit, and I realized what Mom had been talking about. I'd been worried about what my mom was saying about the spells, not what she had called Willow.

"Oh, um, well." I wasn't sure how to explain this one well.

"Did you tell her I was a witch?" Willow's voice had risen quite a bit.

"No, not exactly." I held a hand up, and then ran it through my hair instead. I shuffled my feet a bit, and still couldn't come up with the right words.

Willow stood up straight and put her hands on her hips. The anger transformed her face, and she looked like a fierce Goddess fixing to behead me. I shouldn't have been turned on by that. That absolutely shouldn't have been what my brain was focusing on in this moment.

"Then, *what* exactly?" Her voice had gone cold. Okay. Fire doused.

Realizing I was not getting out of this, I brushed my hand through my hair in worry, trying really hard not to grip the back of the chair like I was going to break it.

"I talked to her the other day about some of the ingredients in the spell." I started to explain.

Willow nodded. "You mentioned that. What does that have to do with it?"

"Well, when she asked who it was for, I said a professor at the college working on a witchcraft book about the history and some spells she had found." I looked away from Willow. "She assumed you were a witch."

"And you didn't correct her, is that it?" Willow's voice was dripping with anger.

"Well, no. I was trying to get information out of her, and it seemed that if that was the assumption she made... I mean, I wasn't ready to introduce you or anything, and it made it easier to deal with her..." And I should have shut up.

Willow's eyes flashed, and I swear I could feel the crackling in the air. If she had been capable of magic, I might be dead. As it stood, I really wanted that invisibility spell at this moment.

"You didn't want to deal with it? So what about when we really are together, and you have to tell your mother? Or are you just going to ask me to lie? Pretend that I'm a witch forever around her, so she doesn't have to convince you otherwise? What about her trying to control my career and what I publish?"

"Willow, it's not –" but she cut me off again.

"No. No, it is. It may not seem like that to you, but you literally lied to your mother, about something you told me did not matter to you—clearly it does. It may have just been an omission of facts, but it made it easier for you now. What will that mean later? Will I always be too hard to explain?"

She took off the apron and tossed it on the table. "I need out of here. I have things to do, anyway. Let me know what mommy dearest says. I'll see you in the morning."

"Willow, please, just let me talk to you."

I reached out, but stopped, knowing I shouldn't invade her space. Waiting to hold her, and apologize until she forgave me.

"Winston... I can't."

Before I could say anything else, Willow was out the door and gone.

I felt utterly defeated. And worse of all, she'd been right. I'd sworn that it hadn't mattered to me she wasn't a witch. That it would not bother me. But I hadn't corrected my mother, even in this small thing, because I hadn't wanted to deal with her. Or have her hold back information she'd have given a witch. I hadn't wanted to hear another lecture about only marrying a witch. I wanted her to care more about *me* than her need for me to carry on our line of witches. I'd known that in falling for Willow, I was doing exactly what my mother did not want. I hadn't been ready to tell her on that phone call. I hadn't wanted to face it. And so I'd taken the easy road.

Willow was right. It showed that I cared about the fact she wasn't a witch in some regard. And if I didn't tell the truth now, if I didn't stand up for her know, would I when it mattered?

I didn't know.

I didn't hear back from my mother that night. Not knowing what to even begin to say to her, I didn't try to call her. My brain wouldn't let go until I texted Willow, though. I just had to apologize again, and ask to see her. She didn't respond either.

She didn't stop by for coffee on her way to work the next morning, and that really made me feel like shit. I didn't think I could feel worse, but I was wrong.

I thought about taking a cup of coffee to her on campus, but even if I asked Charlotte, I worried it was too much of a ploy to get back into her favor. I knew this was much bigger than a cup of coffee could solve.

What would I say?

Then again, she'd blown up so quickly she hadn't really given me a chance to process. And now it looked like she was avoiding me.

And what if she submitted the book?

By afternoon, I was grouchy and hiding in the kitchen. When my phone rang, I expected it to be my mother, but it was my aunt.

I wasn't sure I was up to it, but I answered.

"Winston, my darling boy, what have you done now?"

Taken aback, I stopped what I was doing and paid attention to the phone call. "What?"

"I can feel your unhappiness from here child. Not only that, but your mother has texted me ranting about some love spell, and you and a witch?"

I sighed. Of course, mother would text her. They were sisters after all, but I forgot because they were like night and day. I had no worries my aunt would tell my mother anything I didn't want her to know, though.

I sat the phone down on the table, put it on speaker-phone, and leaned my head into my hands, rubbing my temples.

"Yeah. The first spell we decoded was a kind of love spell. And mother assumed Willow was a witch when I called to ask her questions about ingredients. I danced around it and didn't correct her."

"And Willow found out."

My sigh answered for her.

"My dear boy, you should know better. You'll have to make up for this one." Her voice sounded so gentle and sweet. I decided I needed a cup of tea, and put the kettle on.

"Was it really so bad?" I could hear the pitiful whine in my voice.

"What has Willow been worried about?" my aunt prodded.

"Whether I'll commit to a relationship because she isn't a witch, and…. Shit." I knew it was bad, but I hadn't wanted to face it.

"Shit indeed."

"How do I fix this?"

"Show her you commit, kid. What is the spell?"

"It is supposed to show whether you are soulmates according to the little bit we pieced together. There weren't a lot of directions."

My aunt was silent for a few minutes. "What happened when you two performed the spell together?"

"How did you know we did?"

"I know Willow. Now answer."

Rubbing my temples was doing me no good, but thankfully the kettle whistled. I made some tea and dropped a few drops of my migraine elixir in there.

"Our hands glowed the same color, and I felt a spark of electricity."

"And?"

"And that was what the spell did."

"What happened after that?"

"I... how do you always know when I'm not saying everything?"

"Magic. Now, tell me."

"We slept together. Need more details?"

"Hmmmm."

I took a few sips of my tea. "It was wonderful. Electric. She's all I can think about."

After a pause, she asked, "Had you slept together before that?"

"No. We kissed. We had a conversation about us. But that was it."

"Did the spell do it?" She asked. I took a deep breath and committed to telling her everything.

"Well, we tried again with Willow's friend Piper. Me, and Piper to be exact. I was the same blue glow, but she was red. No aftereffects, no shock, and I didn't try to jump her bones immediately."

"You said you wanted to sleep with Willow before the spell and potion, correct?"

"Yes." I answered simply. She had to have a point.

"Then it wasn't the spell, darling. It may have intensified it, but it wouldn't have put you in bed together. Very few spells can do that, and most are more of a curse. It sounds like it just shows something inside of us that calls like to like. Willow glowed the same color as you, you two just realized what that meant. Simple."

"How do you know that?"

"I used to deep dive into the archives. It's beside the point. Fight your mother on this. And fight for Willow."

"I don't know if she'll forgive me."

"Then work to earn it kiddo. I like Willow, but if you hurt her any more, I might come take the café back. All right, I'm going for a swim. Good luck."

"That's it?"

"Yep. You can do this."

Click.

Work to earn it. Show I could commit. What could I do? If Mother wasn't going to tell me... maybe I could figure it out for myself? But I'd been trying to do that.

Only here, though... not in the archives. Maybe it was time to go home.

Charlotte and the new kid were working the counter, and she was teaching her how to make a drink. I nodded towards Charlotte and pulled her to the side.

"I'm going to talk to Lyzzie tonight, but if I had to leave for a few days, could you handle it here?"

"Absolutely. We did it for your aunt. And we can keep training these two."

"Wonderful. Okay, I'll text you details. Thanks."

"You are coming back though... right?"

Charlotte asked quietly, as I had started to leave. I turned back around.

"What?"

"It's just... Willow hasn't been here. You've seemed upset and distant all day. And I was wondering..."

Ah. She did really like Willow, and had known her much longer than me. Charlotte was also really intuitive.

"Yes, I'm coming back. This is for Willow, even though she doesn't know it yet. Keep the café safe for me, okay?"

She nodded, and I went back to my kitchen to make plans.

I flew home. In less than a day, I was back near the council, ready to confront my mother and get some answers.

My brother was waiting for me. I'd called him, waiting on my flight, so he could pick me up from the airport. That had meant I'd had to fill him in on everything that had happened.

His wife called me an idiot. Brad agreed.

I really couldn't argue.

He didn't hesitate for one second to be there to pick me up though, or to offer to come with me. This late in the evening, mother would be at home. I really wanted to go to the council offices and try to get into the vault for the archives. But I did not know what I was looking for or what exactly my plans were for finding it.

Brad let me take the lead. I left my duffel bag in his backseat, because I wasn't sure I wanted to crash here. With a deep breath, I clenched my hands and knocked on the front door. I could hear footsteps down the hall, and then the bolt being thrown.

Mother's face was shocked when she saw me standing there with Brad behind me. She was still dressed for work, nice dress pants, fancy top, pretty pearl jewelry. Her brown hair was elegantly piled on her head. Mother was always prepared. Unlike before, though, I was too.

She paused, studied me, and quickly "fixed her face" as she always called it. I'm sure the scowl I could feel on my face was not helping matters at all. I clenched my fists to my sides, at the anger I felt. It wasn't all directed at her. No, I wanted to hurt myself a bit too.

"We need to talk. Now." I left no room for argument.

"Whatever it is, is it really that important that you needed to come all the way out here for it? No warning? I mean, I'm happy to see you, but this is a surprise."

"Yes. Yes, it is. I did not want to do this over the phone."

"Could have just sent Brad."

Noticing the side stepping, I shook my head. "Are we going to have this conversation on the porch?"

There was no one to see us. Mother lived in a very nice house with a few acres. A rarity here, but then again, she was on the council and had money. There was even a greenhouse in the back for growing her own herbs. That said, she wouldn't want to take any chances at airing dirty family laundry for all to see.

"No, no. Come on."

She turned and marched down the hallway, spine ram-rod straight as if she'd been called to battle and meant to fight. Her low heels clicked on the tile floor, a sound I remembered with aching clarity from childhood. The room she led me to was our formal living room. And yes, there was an informal one. This one was for important conversations and guests. It was beautifully decorated, dark green tones with wonderfully carved wood furniture. It was like stepping into a forest. I'd loved and hated this room as a kid. Too many dreaded lectures and punishments handed down in here for the aesthetics to fully make up for.

Mother sat in one of the chairs sitting across from the couch. Brad and I both took the couch, and I suddenly remembered many lessons learned as children as we sat exactly like this. My father had passed away when I was young, so Mother had been both roles. She'd excelled in the punishment arena, not so much in the loving, caring, one.

"Is this about the spell or the witch?" she asked, eyebrows raised.

"Both." I said, straight to the point.

"Does she still want to publish them? Really, she has no choice once the council makes a ruling, and we met today about the spells. Surely she'll forgive you and move on."

"You met today about them? You never even called me about the second one."

"No, no, I didn't."

"Mother, you have to tell me what you found." I was gripping my legs, trying to keep from raising my voice.

"No. Simply, I don't."

I growled in frustration. My brother sat a hand on my arm.

"Mother, part of the reason why I came here is to set the record straight. I've made some mistakes I need to fix. That said, I also came here to change your mind, and fight for Willow."

"Is that the witch?"

I growled, "No, actually she isn't a witch."

Mother's face finally changed, showing confusion. "What do you mean, not a witch?"

Brad put his hand up. "Quit the back and forth. Tell her all of it."

And so I did.

Chapter 19

Willow

Winston hadn't messaged me back since that night. He'd sent me a text apologizing, but I knew I wasn't in the right headspace to even try and respond. He hadn't messaged me anything about the spell either. Honestly, I'd be shocked if his mother said anything else at all. She wasn't too forthcoming, so I chalked it up to not having heard anything, and me leaving angry. The next day, I didn't even want fancy coffee. I made some at home and drank it instead.

Tess was worried about me, flying back and forth as I got ready. She knew something had happened the night before, But I had refused to talk about it. I hadn't even called or texted Piper. I just went on about my day and work. With no news from Winston, I decided going by the café would just upset me. I was home in record time. Tess had chilled at the house, and she still looked worried when I showed up, barely even speaking to her.

I finished up grading, and then worked on the manuscript. I wrote what I could on the unfinished spell and my thoughts. If nothing else, I could publish it like this. The soulmate potion chapter was as good as it could be. I couldn't add in the good bits without making this a romance novel and possibly getting fired from my job, so I left out those details. I had a gut feeling that had been all us, but I didn't want to admit it. I dreamed about that night though, over and over.

Those kinds of scenes might sell better than my textbook, and was certainly something to consider later. Maybe I'd write a spicy romance to make extra money. Not sure that it'd count towards my tenure though.

Tess had given up on cheering me up or convincing me to text Piper about it. She'd gone off to work on her own project, and left me some time to cool off. I had to say this kind of anger was doing miraculous things for my work ethic. I'd graded everything I could, worked ahead on a few projects, and started cleaning up the house.

Towards 10 pm, Tess came back into the living room, where I had just finished vacuuming the couch.

"I think you've cleaned enough, Ms. Angry."

"Hey, the house needed it. Don't question my motivations or I'll turn this thing back on your way." I glared, and held up the end of the hose.

Tess floated backward. "Noted, noted. Anyways, it's late. I'm going to bed."

"Same." I sighed. Putting up the vacuum, I turned down the fire, and followed Tess back to the room.

"Going to get coffee in the morning?" She asked, quietly. Almost like she was afraid of me exploding.

I pondered it. I'd had time to cool off. Maybe I should make him seek me out, but why waste a good coffee place in the meantime? I might not even run into him.

"Yes. Night."

"Night!" Tess replied, and she sounded more chipper than she had.

The day dawned, and I dressed with care. I was vain enough to want to make him miss me. I wore one of the original outfits Piper had put together for our "date" that night, a skirt with a pretty top. Of course, it was chilly enough I put on tights, and had a puffy jacket on, so it really didn't matter. But I knew I was hot. Tess thought about coming, but after looking at temps, she changed her mind to stay home.

"Text me when you know something." She said, fluttering by the door.

"Yesh, Tess. I got it. I can handle my love life."

I could hear her suppressed sarcastic comments from the sidewalk after I left. I hurried to the café, looking forward to the warmth of the room and the coffee I could take with me. The leaves had started changing colors, and the sight was glorious. This early in the morning, before the sun had a chance to warm everything up though, it was too chilly to appreciate it.

When I walked in the café Lyzzie looked panicked, then concerned, then worried. She nodded towards me, and it took a few minutes to get to the counter.

"Hey Professor Willow! How are you?" her voice was much peppier than normal, almost more like Charlotte's.

"Doing well. You look swamped. Where's Winston?"

"Oh, um. He was just busy with something is all."

"Oh. I had a question for him. I might..."

Lyzzie threw her hands up. "No, no. No need for that. I'm sure you can ask later. Or text him. Or I can leave a note?"

I paused, watching her. She was jumpy and very nervous for some reason. I decided to start around the corner.

"Willow, aren't you going to be late for class?" she asked.

I looked up at the clock, which read 8:30. She knew I never taught this early.

"Lyzzie... what's going on?"

And she caved, her whole body sinking inwards.

"Okay, so Winston left yesterday afternoon."

"What?" I felt blindsided by that one. I blinked my eyes a few times.

"He said he had to go do something. He promised he's coming back, though." Lyzzie held up her hands, "Promise. We asked him point blank."

I let that sink in. Where could he have gone? Back home? Was he running because of the fight? Had I overreacted?

It hadn't felt like it at the time... but love does stupid things to you. And losing it is worse. Maybe... was he coming back? Would he have lied to them?

"Okay. Thanks for letting me know."

"Yeah, of course. He should be back tomorrow. Seriously. I'm sure you'll hear from him."

I just nodded, holding up my coffee in thanks, and heading back out into the cold. It felt nice now, cooling down my burning cheeks and flushed body under my clothes.

Embarrassed and unsure of myself, I wished I hadn't had to teach. No one there would know though, and they did not like us to cancel our classes. Teach I must, even if I felt like a complete loser. I drank the coffee, not enjoying it as much as usual, and tried to pay attention to my walk.

He left.

Why did he leave? Because of me? That made little sense. I had nonstop questions running through my head: What would have required him leaving for me? Was he talking to his mother? Breaking into the council chamber? Running away because he'd realized he could never be with me and didn't want to face the conversation?

Thoughts kept running through my head nonstop. It was a circling train of chaos, and when Tess texted for an update, I simply told her "later". Once I was able to dive into work, I did better. Not great, but better. A few students noticed how distracted I was, asking if I felt well, but I managed for the most part.

I did not stop at the café on my way home. Maybe I should swear off bread and coffee altogether. That thought was quickly brushed to the side—no man was worth losing coffee or bread over.

My home was rather lit up when I got there, and as soon as I opened the door, I knew why.

Tess had given up on me, and called in reinforcements.

Music played, the fire burned, and something delicious was being made in my kitchen. Piper was already here.

I dropped my bag, and she swooped in from the side and hugged me, Tess alighting on my shoulder. I soaked in the hug and cried for the first time since the fight. This was silly, and insane, and I couldn't help that my heart ached in a way I had never felt before.

"Oh honey. I'm so sorry." Piper said, rubbing my back. She pulled me forward, and closed the door behind me.

"It's okay. It'll be okay. We weren't even like officially dating." I muttered through tears.

Piper pulled back and looked me over. "Want me to punch him?

"I can jab him in the eye!" Tess shouted in glee.

I laughed and shook my head. "I don't even know for sure where he went."

"Went? What do you mean? He's not at the café?"

"No. Lyzzie told me this morning he'd gone. He should be back tomorrow."

"To do what?" Tess asked.

"I have no idea."

"Then you also don't know what his intentions were. Maybe it's not as bad as you think. Maybe he had good reasons." Piper leaned back, and let go of me. I sat my bag down and took off my coat.

"Maybe. But I sure don't feel like pinning my hopes on that. No offense."

"As you shouldn't. Go sit. Tess can keep you company while I plate our dinners."

There were no words for having friends like this. I went and sat down as I was bid, and pulled the cover up and around me. Tess landed on the arm of the couch, stealing a bit of the blanket for her legs.

Her iridescent purple wings fluttered slowly. I leaned my head back on the couch, and watched. I'd always loved her wings and wished for a pair of my own. What wonders one would be able to see if they could fly. You could travel, see so many sights.

Before long, Piper hollered at Tess, who flew away. They both came back, Tess carrying her own little plate and bowl, and Piper with two in her hands. She sat them down on the coffee table, where a wine bottle and glasses were already sitting.

The smell was amazing. Piper had made pasta, with rolls sitting on the plate beside the bowl. I breathed in deeply and smiled.

"Chicken Alfredo?"

"My specialty."

We pulled on the coffee table top, and it raised to a good level for eating on the couch. The pasta was rich and hot. It tasted as good as it smelled, and I reveled in the flavor. With a sauce that was thick and creamy, it tasted of garlic and parmesan. The chicken was tender and flavorful all on its own. Pasta was right up there with bread and coffee.

"How much did you make?" I asked.

"Plenty to leave you leftovers. I saw the sad state of your fridge."

"Hey, we just went shopping!"

"For frozen meals and lunchables."

"True. Never a better friend could I have."

She laughed, and said, "One of us had to learn how to cook, or we never would have survived."

"I would have survived. I had coffee."

"Coffee would not have kept you alive. Or fast food. I remember how you ate in college. Bleh."

It was my turn to laugh, and the joy felt good. Tess shook her head.

"You could just forage for berries and such."

"You look like you're foraging quite a lot right now." I raised my eyebrow.

"I'm just saying to survive. I'm not doing it unless I have to."

We turned on a baking show then and ate the food. I got up and got us a second helping, and more rolls. By the end of the show, my heart felt lighter. It still hurt, but I didn't feel like I was being crushed.

"Do you want to talk about it?" Piper asked.

I shrugged. "What is there to talk about? You already know the details."

"Only as relayed by Tess, and you didn't tell her much. Today, as a matter of fact, you sent 'later' and she rightly panicked and called me in."

I sighed and nodded. "We were having trouble figuring out the second spell. Winston was close and decided we should call his mom. I debated, but gave in. From there, it all went to hell."

"I can imagine. I've met the woman once. She's fierce."

Trying to imagine Winston's mother got me nowhere. I shook my head to dispel the image.

"She said she'd look for information the first time he talked to her, but upon hearing about the first spell, she demanded he tell his 'witch' that I could not publish it. She kept referencing me that way. We hadn't told her I was there when Winston called her, he'd just put her on speakerphone.."

"Witch? That's why you fought?"

"Yeah, that's why we fought. When he was first telling her about what he was doing, she assumed I was a witch since I was writing about, and working in the field."

"Not a bad assumption as they go. You are about the only non-witch I know who does."

I nodded, "True, but he apparently decided she'd be easier to deal with if he didn't tell her, and did not correct the mistake."

"Ouch. Did he use those words when he told you?" Piper looked shocked.

"Yep. Or started to, he cut himself off towards the end."

She looked down at her empty bowl. "Well. I can't say I blame you for getting angry."

"After all that talk about him not caring if I was a witch or not, and that it didn't matter what his kids were, witches or not... and then he let his mother assume I was so he didn't have to argue. Will he ever want to argue the point? What about the next time someone assumes that about me? And was it really because he does want a witch for a wife?"

Tess flew up into my face. "You know, parents can be the worst."

And that was the kicker. Because I knew what it was like to lie to your parents to avoid a fight.

"Yeah, yeah they can. I can't even be mad about that part really. I get him not wanting to fight with his mother. From what he said before, they've been having a rocky few months anyways."

Piper stayed quiet. She knew that I'd lied to my parents about what I was studying at the university because they would never have helped me do it.

"Maybe he's flown home to set the record straight." she suggested.

"Lyzzie just said that he was doing something for me—and he promised he'd be back."

"Will you talk to him when he comes back?"

I looked at my bag by the door, thinking of my laptop, the manuscript, and the book I planned to send to my agent—with the spells—soon.

"Yeah. But I'm not sure it'll be a happy talk."

"You can only try, Willow. And I know the book is important to you... but if publishing something could mean losing the support of the witch community, you need to think about that too. You've fought hard for your place here. Don't jeopardize that."

There was weight to that argument that I had not thought of. Though we lived together, mostly in harmony with witches, there was a lot of pushback against a non-witch being so involved in their history and magic. Many thought that I could not understand it, or that I would rewrite it to fit a narrative. Winston's aunt had actually played a key role in helping me get my position in the first place. I needed their overall support to keep doing what I was doing. I couldn't teach the history of magic with no witches supporting me.

It'd never been about the prestige I could get from the witches.. It'd been about my love for it, and the witches who had been so kind to me growing up. It'd been about what I couldn't stand other people saying or believing about people I had loved. It'd been about sharing the truth of their history, and making non-magical folk understand it too.

No one deserved such hatred, simply for being the way they were born.

We spent the rest of the night watching baking shows and laughing. Piper and Tess kept me distracted until we were all so tired that Piper called it a night and headed home. Tess went to her tiny house, and I changed into pajamas and collapsed into bed to see what the next few days brought.

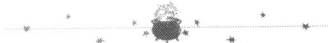

The answer was not much. I taught, graded, and finished a read through on the book. Because the second spell wasn't finished, I decided to turn it into a lesson about lost history and magic. That in our determination to persecute others, we'd lost valuable skills to the ages. Perhaps there were consequences to any type of spell, and we all knew that some spells could be used for nefarious means. Even then, it didn't also negate the good that such spells could bring. I enjoyed writing it.

I left in the soul mate spell.

If the witches' council had someone who could pull it in the publishing stage, so be it. If they wanted to speak with me themselves, they could. I'd be more than happy to have an actual conversation about it, and the decisions they were making. Otherwise, I'd just pretend I'd misunderstood Winston, or say he hadn't passed the information along. I'd already written a note to my editor about it, and the agent, so they could be prepared.

I still had time before I had to send it in though, so I waited. Waiting for Winston.

And then on Sunday, I got a text.

"I'm back. And we really need to talk. Come to the café? Let me apologize in person. Please."

I was sitting at home working with Tess on a project for her house. She stopped, and just said, "Go."

So I went.

I didn't change, I didn't get fancy. I had no desire to make him regret me. I just wore my sweats, with my hair pulled back, and an old gray t-shirt that said "Pivot." Sexy.

Winston was waiting for me, sitting at the kitchen table and staring at the door.

When I walked through, he stood and stayed still. The room smelled of fresh baked bread and peppermint, heaven in a bottle. There was barely a sound, and the door closing behind me nearly made me jump out of my skin.

I watched him as he watched me. My body still felt pulled to him. All I wanted was to run into his arms, have him hold me and then cart me off to bed. Did all of this really matter?

But sadly, the answer was yes. And so, I waited for him to speak.

Chapter 20

Winston

My time in California hadn't been wasted. On the flight back to the café, I'd been lost in thought, thinking of what to say to Willow, and how to apologize. I knew part of this going forward was earning her trust again.

I thought back on that moment when I'd told my mother everything that had happened. Of Willow, and what kind of woman she was. Strong, intelligent, beautiful. Of what we had done with the spell already.

My mother had been furious at first. The anger had radiated from her, and I'd been worried she was going to confine me to my room and make sure I never left again. I was thankful for my brother. He'd been a rock, sure and strong, not moving in the face of her arguments, which were many. I shouldn't marry a nonmagical person who was clearly obsessed with magic - she'd started the relationship by using me, and would never stop. Why couldn't I consider Willow's best friend instead? Wouldn't I regret these choices I was making? How dare I perform a spell with a nonmagical person, when I wasn't even sure of what it would do?

To be fair, she'd had a few fair points on that last bit.

My brother counteracted the more irrelevant ones. The fact that my brother already had children with a witch, who were witches, had helped. The legacy was at least safe guarded to continue. What did I matter? Not a pretty argument when you think about it in those terms, but one we made regardless.

My aunt had been the final nail in the coffin of defeating my mother's arguments. She'd called and informed my mother that she was being ridiculous. Good things would come from this if I didn't screw it up, and if my mother didn't as well. After telling my mother to shut it for the final time (her words, not mine), she'd launched into her own idea of what we should do.

That idea had led to me staying in California longer than I intended. I'd thought about calling or texting Willow... to let her know that I wasn't ignoring her. But I hadn't known what to say until I could give her all of it. So I'd held off and hoped and prayed she'd still be willing to speak to me once I'd returned. I'd messaged both Charlotte and Lyzzie daily to check on the café and let them know a timeline of when I was returning. Other than that, I'd stayed busy.

The flight home wasn't enough time to mentally prepare myself for everything. Yet my heart couldn't wait any longer. I'd gone far too many days without seeing Willow. I'd even googled her picture on the university webpage to show my mother and brother... and saved it to my phone.

I landed early in the day, and went straight to the café. The place was booming, but Charlotte and the new hire had it under control. Charlotte beamed at me, but relayed the story of Willow stopping in that first morning, and that they hadn't seen her since. I thanked her and went to the kitchen. I put in a loaf of prepared bread in the oven, and then went upstairs to the apartment to shower and make myself presentable.

Then I texted Willow.

And when "On my way" came through, I nearly locked myself in the bathroom in panic. Instead, I went to the kitchen, lit a candle, and waited.

Willow walked through the café door looking tired, and I felt a sadness that I had been a part of that. She was beautiful, though, and it took all my willpower not to rush over and kiss her in greeting. Never mind the sweats and ponytail, she looked as hot as any other day I had seen her.

I had to do this right. I needed to wipe away that hurt and pain from her eyes.

I'd baked bread as soon as I got back, and set a peppermint candle burning. I could see her slightly smile as she stood there, and I knew she liked it. When the door closed, with a very loud click in the silence, she jumped a little.

A smile crossed my lips at that. I realized we were still standing in silence and gathered all the courage I had found over the past few days.

"First, I must apologize. I should have corrected my mother. No matter how much of a pain she can be, it was wrong to let her think something of you that was not true. It will never happen again. No matter how much my mother and I fight, there was no excuse for it, and I was wrong. That said, I also want to further apologize for all future dealings with my mother... because I know her.

"I promise I have no qualms in being with you because you are not a witch. I do not care. I think of nothing but you, from the moment I wake to the moment I sleep, and even in my dreams. You are with me and have been present in all my thoughts and desires, every second of every moment, since the first time I laid eyes on you. If such a thing as soulmates exist, then I know you are mine, and I am yours. I did not need a spell to confirm it."

I could hear Willow breathe in deeply, and I walked forward a bit.

"Willow, I love you. I know we haven't known each other long, and I know there is still so much I can learn about you. But it doesn't change how I feel, no matter how much I fought it because of my past. I ran away from being pressured into a relationship I didn't want for my mother. I didn't want to run headlong into one either. But it never felt like that, it never felt wrong with you."

Willow shook her head. "Then why did you leave?"

"I went to see my mother. She hadn't responded back to me about the spell. And I had a lovely aunt who was kind to call and knock some sense into me."

At that Willow smiled. She knew Maggie well enough to know what that had been like.

"I knew I'd never have a fair argument with my mother on the phone. I also knew that you needed answers, and the best place for me to get that was in California. You didn't want to speak to me, and I didn't blame you. So I went to earn you back."

Willow started to shake her head at this, but I kept going. "I explained who you are, what you are to me. I told her I was wrong to let her think otherwise. My brother went as well and fought with me. He supports us, and together... well, I won't say my mother is happy that I am not with a witch—I won't lie to you. But between my brother, me, and my aunt calling, she's realized she no longer has a say. And that's more than I can say about our past arguments."

Willow started to talk, but I held up a hand, and said, "Wait. There's more."

I picked up a manilla envelope that had been on the table. "This is all the research my mother found on both spells. We figured out the rest of the second spell. And I got my mother to relent on the first one being published."

Willow audibly gasped at that one.

"What? How?"

"Well, my aunt helped with that one. She had already come up with a plan after talking to me. Intuition has always been her best magic, and she knew I'd need help. We all did the spell. My brother and sister-in-law volunteered to do it together, thankfully they glowed the same. Then we pulled in some random groupings of people - none of whom were in a relationship already. No one else glowed the same, except for a random couple my aunt tried on the cruise.

"Were there different colors?" She asked, intrigued.

"Yes. Colors of the rainbow. Mainly though, my point being, it um, didn't have the same effects on people as it did you and me, except for the same or different glowing hands."

Willow looked down at her hands, and a blush crept up her chest and cheeks.

"Just us, huh?"

"I think that had more to do with the fact that I wanted to devour you from the moment we touched. My brother has been with his wife for years, and they have cooled off a bit, so he says they might have done it in their prime."

Willow laughed. "I might need to add that bit to the warnings."

I laughed a little too. "I'd appreciate keeping the rest out of it."

"Oh, I don't know. A good spice scene might sell my textbook to students at a much higher rate."

I choked a little, and she laughed harder.

"I'm kidding, I'm kidding. Gosh, the department would kill me. It's okay."

Taking a chance, I walked closer to her. I gave her the folder of information. "I'm sorry. I'll do whatever I can to make it up to you, from this day forward, if you will forgive me, and give me another chance. Willow, I love you, and I want to keep loving you for the rest of our days."

Willow's eyes shimmered with unshed tears, and she looked down for a minute. Then she looked up at me and took the last step needed to fully close the distance between us. I could feel her body pressed up against mine.

She smiled, slow and mischievous, and said, "I have a few ideas to start."

And I was lost, once again.

I was against her in a second, kissing her with all the pent up worry I had had for the past few days. I'd dreamed of nothing but her, and now I wanted to do all the things I had been fantasizing about.

Her arms wrapped around my neck, going into my hair and grabbing. I felt her up against me, and my body responded. She groaned, and I decided we should vacate the kitchen before we had a repeat of the first time.

I pulled back and looked at her flushed face. With a smile, I pulled her hand from my hair and took her with me upstairs. She followed without saying a word.

In my bedroom, I turned her around against the bed, and leaned into her again. I started nibbling down her neck and decided there were just way too many layers between me and her skin. With a few quick motions, I had her top off.

"Sorry, no cute bra this time," Willow said. She seemed embarrassed.

"That is really the last thing on my mind right now," I said, leaning into her. She could feel how much I wanted her.

"Trust me," and I went back to kissing her all over, as I unhooked her bra and it joined the rest of the clothes. Then I dropped and started pulling off her pants. Her moans urged me on, and when I licked the top of her thigh, she grabbed my hair again, and held me there. I eased her back onto the bed, and began apologizing in the best way I could.

When she had orgasmed twice, she pulled on me, and moaned out "in me. Now. Please."

"As my lady commands." I said and kissed my way up her body to her mouth. As I kissed her again, I plunged into her, thrusting and creating that glorious tension in both of us. As I got close to coming, I slowed down. She growled at me, her nails digging into my shoulders.

"Shh, I want you to come again," I said, kissing her mouth once more. Then I plunged hard, over and over, and as she came, I did too.

I lowered myself off to the side, and she rolled over and curled into me.

"That was a good first apology," she said, her voice almost a purr.

"I'll work on making the second one great," I said, and she groaned at me.

"Sleep first. At least a nap."

I laughed and pulled her even closer against me, wrapping my arms around her. She was tucked against me, and I tucked her head under my chin. She cuddled against me, snuggling, and I grabbed the blanket on the side to cover us. Within a minute, she was breathing in a way that let me know she was sleeping. I closed my eyes and just soaked in the feeling of happiness and perfection I felt holding her. She fit against me like she had always been meant to be there.

I awoke in the middle of the night and watched Willow for a minute, remembering everything that had happened. With a smile, I started kissing her, gently, slowly, and with the utter worship I felt for her body. When she moved slightly, I knew she had awoken. She let out a little moan that lit me up.

With intention, I kissed every inch of her body, from her face down to her feet, and started my way back up. Her skin was warm from being under the blanket, and I could feel her flesh responding to my touch. Willow reached out to me, dragging me back up to her, and kissed me, deep and long. Her hands ran down my body and grabbed my shaft, rubbing up and down.

I growled into the kiss and pulled back. "I'm supposed to be apologizing to you here."

"You can't have all the fun," she whispered back, and shimmied down before I knew what she was doing. When I felt her lick the tip of me, I nearly fell on top of her. I groaned as she continued to use her mouth on me. It was a strain to hold myself up and keep myself from yanking her back up.

With my own deep moan, I finally pulled away and got off the bed. I grabbed her legs and pulled her to the end of the bed, spreading her legs as I did.

"My turn."

I lowered myself to my knees and licked up her thigh. Then the other. I could hear her gasping. Looking up at her, I made my way to the center of her, and began apologizing in earnest. Based on the noises she was making, I was certainly on my way to being forgiven.

"Winston, if you don't stop now and fuck me, I'm going to be too ramped up to do it," Willow growled, and I responded immediately.

We moved together, bringing us both to the edge, and then together over it. I watched her as we tumbled together and knew this was who I wanted to be with for the rest of my life.

I lay down beside her, and brushed her hair from her face. She turned to me, running her own fingers through my hair, and kissing me gently on the lips.

"I love you, Willow. I know we've only known each other for a short time, but there is no doubt in my mind that I want to be with you forever."

"I love you, Winston."

We kissed again, sweetly and slowly. I pulled the cover back over us once again. Then together, we both passed to the land of dreams, knowing that tomorrow, we'd have each other.

When my alarm went off at 5 am that morning, I heard Willow groan.

"If that has to continue, I may never stay the night here again. Or I might murder you. One or the other."

"Noted." I laughed, turning off the alarm, and stretched. She jolted out of bed.

"I have to send in the manuscript. I've got to look over all of this and fix it. Oh, I have classes today. I've got to go."

I barely had time to process any of this before she was up, dressed, and nearly out the door. Bleary-eyed, I followed, and she turned back around. She pecked me on the lips, said "Thanks, text you later," and was gone.

She hadn't even had coffee.

Charlotte had apparently told Lyzzie something about yesterday, and she just held a thumbs up at me when I walked out.

I didn't even want to know what they had discussed. I also had the sudden urge to make sure my room upstairs was soundproofed.

Chapter 21

Willow

I had finished the manuscript. It'd been set, ready to go. Yet I still had time to make a few changes to it because of what Winston had found and done. I poured over the contents of the envelope. It gave me new history on the spells, along with wording and better instructions. His mother may not have wanted to help, but she had surely provided excellent research. I almost wanted to meet her.

Almost.

I did want to hug Maggie and tell her how thankful I was for what she had done. That I'd hopefully get to do sooner rather than later.

After Winston's doomed alarm had gone off, I'd run home, quickly got ready and filled in Tess as I did so, then ran to campus. I hadn't even paused for coffee. This was the most energized I had felt in years. Before and in between classes, I worked on the book, and tweaked not only the ending, but the beginning and those two tricky chapters with the spells themselves. He hadn't mentioned the second spell when he'd spoken to me yesterday much, but the contents had been inside the envelope. I could only assume that meant I had permission.

The final product was something I was extremely proud of. I emailed it to my agent, who had sent me a worried email that morning. The reply was exhilarating to send, as it contained the full manuscript, illustrations, and my excited hope that it would be published on schedule as well.

This week had been student midterms. I'd crushed many hearts who hadn't studied. It was a mix of multiple choice, and two essays. I'd been generous and given them a list of 5 historical events, like the Salem Witch Trials, to study—and papers varied on which they got. If they studied... they'd do well.

Classes were done for the day, and the evening was falling. The days were getting shorter, night falling faster, and the cold chill creeping back in. I really needed to remember never to have a deadline around midterms again. Looking forward to the rest of the semester, now that the book was in, I'd be grading these essays for probably the next week or two.

Grading, when all I really wanted to do was spend every waking moment with Winston. It felt like I had fallen head over heels, and had no hope of anything else. I'd been lost in a dream, rudely awoken for a bit, and then quite quickly fallen back asleep to drift in a sea of love.

Did I care? No, I really didn't. Soulmates. Could we really be soulmates? We'd known each other for 20 days, and in those 20 days I'd fallen in love. He'd flown across the country to confront his mother and help me. To prove that he'd known he'd hurt me, but he would do anything to make it up to me.

He'd been working on that well last night, too.

My whole body warmed, and looking out the window, I decided I needed to head back to the café. I'd meet up with Winston, then go home and check on Tess. There'd be so many conversations to have eventually: living arrangements, Tess, the café and my career.

All things to worry about later. For now, it was time to go. I filed all the essays away into my backpack with my laptop, turned off the coffee pot, and flipped off the light. With a click, the door was shut and locked, and I was rushing out of the building.

When I approached the café, the lights were glowing warmly inside. I could hear the classical music playing, and I was thankful for this space that I had loved for years now, being even more part of my life. The smell of coffee drifted on the air, and the crisp evening chill made me bundle my scarf tighter.

Charlotte was inside with the new hire, Marcus, and I waved at both of them as I went to the kitchen in the back. Winston turned around, covered in flour, and smiling.

"Welcome back. I thought you'd be here earlier."

I dropped my backpack by the table and breathed in the wonderful smells.

"Happy to be back. Submitted the book, and gave all my midterms. Besides, maybe some grading, I'm done for the night. And sorry - I should have texted."

"No worries! I'm just getting this last batch of cookies ready to go. We can eat here soon, if you want?"

"Lovely. I'll go grab coffee, and grade then."

Winston shook his head and laughed at me, but didn't mention my coffee habit. Maybe I'd try to cut back, just a little.

Piper texted me soon after. She quizzed me about all the details and threatened to come to the café to get me to talk. I readily agreed to the plan, and twenty minutes later she was at the door and waiting. I commandeered Winston's apartment, and we headed up.

"Well this is a cozy little spot." Piper said as she made herself home on the couch.

I shook my head, sitting at the little table across the way. "It is."

"Okay, tell me, tell me everything."

I did, and we laughed, and delighted in the story. She took a wicked delight in asking me for all the good moments.

"So, it's all okay? You forgive him?"

I looked down at my hands, and then around the space. Thinking carefully about my answer before I just blurted out a yes.

"I do. You know I've lied to my parents to avoid difficult conversations. I haven't actually met his mother, but from his stories and what happened, I can see that it was a gut reaction on his part to just go along with it. I don't think he thought it through, really. I..."

I paused, really thinking this through. Piper waited patiently.

"Because of past experiences, I was ready to think the worst, you know? I expected him to really care that I wasn't a witch. I had a hard time believing him when he said he didn't. But he went above and beyond to show how much he cares about me—,"

"I'll say," Piper cut in. I ignored her.

"And I love him." I finished simply.

"You do?" Piper looked so happy.

"I do. If soulmates are real, we must be."

Winston came up then, and knocked on the door. When we said enter he poked his head and asked if Piper wanted to stay for dinner. I insisted, and so we trooped down to the kitchen to eat together. It was a wonderful meal, and a great time seeing that Piper and Winston would get along too. Tess wasn't here, but Piper was going to swing by and take her to her house tonight.

Perhaps there was something I could do for Piper... I owed so much of my happiness now to her and Tess.

What would the future hold? I didn't know for sure. But looking into Winston's eyes, I knew that I was happy with where my life held. And I really wish I could meet the witch responsible for hiding those two spells. I owed her more than she could ever realize.

Chapter 22

Epilogue

The café was humming. It was finals week, and all the students were gathering together to study as snow blanketed the world outside. Many had found out about the place from Willow and their new friends working there. It was keeping us busy, and me baking. Willow pitched in to help a little, but spent most of her time in the kitchen grading, or out at a table with some students discussing their final projects.

Watching her work and interacting with others brought me joy. It never failed that she was kind and considerate, and even if she complained about her students not reading emails or instructions, she always painstakingly replied to them. I'd had to hide her phone a couple of times, just to keep her from checking her email again late at night. We had other plans, and I needed her full attention.

She'd gotten word back that the book was fully accepted, and through editing. Because of the timeline, we were supposed to be sent a proof this weekend, or so she thought. A box had arrived today for her, and I was ready to surprise her.

Piper came by often every evening as well, and had teased us both incessantly. She'd also joked about me finding a friend for her.

Overall, I couldn't believe that my whim of taking over this café from my aunt had led to all of this. I was the happiest that I had ever been. My soul was light, my heart was full, and I finally felt like I had made peace with my mother. My brother planned to visit over the holidays, and I couldn't wait to show him everything.

What a whirlwind it had been.

Finals week wrapped. It was a semester of challenges and near heartbreak, but it was more than anything, one of the best in my life. Winston was still apologizing every night, and between that and my book successfully being submitted for publication, I was happy. Happy and in love, and more content than I had ever been in my life.

That night, I came up to the apartment after graduation, tired but happy. Winston was at the table, a meal prepared for both of us, candles glowing on the cabinets and shelves, and soft piano music playing in the background.

I stopped short, throwing my graduation robe on the couch. I pulled the tam from my head and tossed it there, too. "Winston?"

"I know I cook for you all the time, but I thought that I'd add a bit more romance to our night. Soon, I hope we can go on a proper date. But this arrived... and I wanted to celebrate it with you."

He held out a box marked proof with my name on it. With a gasp and a racing heart, I took it and pulled the tab on it. Out came a beautiful hardback book, with his illustrations on it, and the title "*Lost Spells and Witchcraft History: A Journey Through Time*—by Willow Redwine" on it. I flipped the pages, seeing the glossy images and drawings for the first time. It was better than anything I had ever done.

"Oh, Winston, it's beautiful."

He smiled and said "Congratulations."

I flipped back to the dedication page and held it out to him.

"To Winston—for whom this book sings. My soulmate, my illustrator, and the one who helped make all this possible."

He smiled softly, set the book aside, and grabbed me by the waist, pulling me to him.

"I think supper can wait."

"Oh, really?"

"Yes. Wanna wear the tam? You're kind of cute in it."

I laughed, and he pulled me back to the bedroom. I didn't know what I had done to deserve all of this, but I silently thanked whatever witch had left hidden those spells and hoped her life had been as lucky.

A partnership, a problem, and a passion are blooming... and maybe love.

Piper excels at her job alone, but now she's been assigned a new temporary partner – an extremely arrogant Elf. To top it all off, he's hot, and passionate about saving nature making Piper forget whether she wants to hit him or kiss him.

Deals & Dalliances Cover

River has often gone against Elven tradition, but he's always fought for the Earth. Now he's been assigned to work with a witch to help secure more land. She may drive him crazy first, especially since all he thinks about are better uses for her lips.

Will the two of them realize there's more than just physical attraction? Can they stop arguing long enough to see they may be falling for each other?

In Deals & Dalliances, you'll find dual first-person points of view of a magical health environmentalist and a park ranger. Magic, enemies to lovers, and a little more spice.

Willow's Peppermint Mocha

1 double shot espresso

1/2 cup steamed milk (of choice)

2 pumps chocolate syrup

2 pumps peppermint syrup

Top with a generous portion of whipped cream the sprinkle with crushed candy canes (or peppermint wheels).

Add a candy cane "stirrer" as garnish, if you'd like.

Want a bonus short story about how Tess and Willow met?
Subscribe to my newsletter:

Thank you All!

There are so many people I want to thank, and I know I will never be able to remember all of them, or list them all. So just know that if you helped me along in this journey, thank you.

I thanked this group in the beginning but I wanted to share more information about them. I attend many writing conferences and events through The Writer's Sanctuary which is run by CJ Redwine and Mary Weber! They are great events, where I have met and created a wonderful writing tribe and learned more than I can express. I'm also a member of The Red Herrings Society – which does cost a monthly fee but you get two free teachings, access to the Facebook group, we do write ins, and hang out, plus bonus information. If you wish to learn more about those, see here: https://the-writers-sanctuary.com/

Scan here for TWS Web-site

To my family – my mom, husband, son, sister, and others, who have been so supportive through this journey! Thank you.

To my author community, especially the amazing ones I've met on TikTok and become friends with. I could never manage to thank all of you as needed. Huge shout out to Heather K. Carson who has been amazing in walking me through steps and issues that come up, answering all kinds of questions, and just all around being awesome. (Go check out her books – https://www.amazon.com/s tores/Heather-K.-Carson/author/B0BVSRMFYK)

To my professor, who has helped me with my creative writing goals – and bought me Atticus so that I could format books.

To my cover designer, Aaricia Wiesen of Malice & Mayhem Book Covers, thank you so much for creating such a beautiful cover. You can find her on Facebook& @mm-bookcovers on Instagram.

Last but certainly never least, thank you so much to my readers, my beta readers, my arc readers, and you, for finding this book and giving it a chance. Thank you. I'd appreciate a review (Amazon and Goodreads!) but in no way expect it.

Quirky, creative, and always weird - I strive to be authentically me and help others to do their best. Born and raised in Kentucky, I married my high school sweetheart, Sean, and we have one son named Xander. I'm a college professor, teaching First Year Experience (The how to college and adult class), and Organizational Leadership. I absolutely love what I do, and am so thankful to also have the time to pursue my writing dream.

Find me at: https://www.fallonwilloughby.com/

Scan the code above code to see the website, my books and sign up for my newsletter!

19477741R00181